5/00

THE DRY DANUBE

Also by Paul West

Fiction

Life With Swan
Terrestrials
Sporting With Amaryllis
The Tent of Orange Mist
Love's Mansion
The Women of Whitechapel and Jack the Ripper
Lord Byron's Doctor
The Place in Flowers where Pollen Rests
The Universe, and Other Fictions
Rat Man of Paris
The Very Rich Hours of Count von Stauffenberg
Gala
Colonel Mint
Caliban's Filibuster
Bela's Lugosi's White Christmas
I'm Expecting to Live Quite Soon
Alley Jaggers
Tenement of Clay

Nonfiction

My Mother's Music
A Stroke of Genius
Sheer Fiction – Volumes I, II, III
Portable People
Out of My Depths: A Swimmer in the Universe
Words for a Deaf Daughter
I, Said the Sparrow
The Wine of Absurdity
The Snow Leopard
The Modern Novel
Byron and the Spoiler's Art
James Ensor
The Spellbound Horses

THE DRY DANUBE

A Hitler Forgery

•

PAUL WEST

A New Directions Book

Book design by Erik Rieselbach
Manufactured in the United States of America
New Directions Books are printed on acid-free paper.
First published clothbound in 2000
Published simultaneously in Canada by Penguin Books Canada Limited
Published by arrangement with Paul West and his agent, Elaine Markson, New York

Library of Congress Cataloging-in-Publication Data
West, Paul, 1930–
The Dry Danube: a Hitler forgery / by Paul West.
p.   cm.
ISBN 0-8112-1432-X (acid-free paper)
1. Hitler, Adolf, 1889–1945 — Homes and haunts — Austria — Vienna — Fiction.
2. Hitler, Adolf, 1889–1945 — Childhood and youth — Fiction.
3. Teacher-student relationships — Austria — Vienna — Fiction.
4. Literary forgeries and mystifications — Fiction.
5. Art students — Austria — Vienna — Fiction. 6. Vienna (Austria) — Fiction.
I. Title.
PS3573.E8247 D7 2000
813'.54–dc21   99-088020

New Directions Books are published for James Laughlin
by New Directions Publishing Corporation,
80 Eighth Avenue, New York 10011

Contents

THE DRY DANUBE

Until I at last wearied

UNTIL I AT LAST WEARIED of Treischnitt's skies, I peered at them daily, that old master's, at their texture and their hint of third dimension, having no inkling of how much I would eventually peer at Kolberhoff's houses, which always looked different when viewed right after peering at Treischnitt's skies, as was also true for Kolberhoff's houses. It was all a matter of context, even if the Treischnitt sky I was peering at was in a painting that contained no house at all, and vice versa. The only true context, I told myself, was in the mind of the beholder. Treischnitt died before Kolberhoff, of course, being older, but they had both vanished from my ken before I realized I would never know them intimately. I had always hoped, even in my salad days, not to be lethally disregarded by those who mattered to me. So Treischnitt died, much given to anger in his last years, not Kolberhoff, their works persisting in my head, neither living nor dead, but neutrally exact. It would have been the

3

same if Kolberhoff, genial to the last, had gone first, before Treischnitt, except that in the end Kolberhoff might have been thinking he would precede Treischnitt, thus *condemning* Treischnitt to a Kolberhoffless world. It was in their works they died first. There is a death each time you lay down paint and it dries amid the rough ownership of your gaze. Only those who have not eaten too large a portion of life can remain happy with their work; they always have something to look forward to. So if it was not skies it was houses and on red-letter days houses below skies, skies above houses in the decent balance the illustrative artist aspires to. After all, you are only transferring the stuff of one world to another place in the same world. These truths came to me early, but I won no credit for them, indeed receiving many mouthfuls of renegade insult about my lacking the power of mutilation. You cannot have everything, not even in later years when, picking a point and a place, you consider how you have fared. You may not be able to do this later, for grotesque reasons. So, with Treischnitt and Kolberhoff missing, and their works a blur of buried secrets—How could either of them be that good?—I learned how to look at the space behind a canvas, seeing nothing at all, though conceding the obvious presence of a wall or a fireplace. If their work no

4

longer detains you, you miss them less, whom you never got to know anyway, they being somewhat standoffish whether in bad or good temper. They were not clavier chords. Sometimes one must practice a mental hygiene based on self-saving ardor. When those who claim to know refuse to make the rest move over, then you have to minister to yourself, making sweet calm where you might have been as cranky as Treischnitt, or Kolberhoff imitating him so as not to seem a softie. Oh, the murder in their hearts as they failed to take their critics with them into finality, as in some old song of saying farewell to the world that has bruised you so. No matter: I linger on these men. With what hesitation I had left for Treischnitt a crumpled little postcard of some Italian lake, popped on his stoop like a hostage. It would have been amazing if he had concluded it came from anyone at all rather than having been blown there on the wind, willed to embarrass him by Kolberhoff. It was only after I had wooed Treischnitt with another postcard, signed with my initials, and then a little water color of my own, unsigned, that I turned to Kolberhoff. I left more for Treischnitt than for Kolberhoff, having started with Treischnitt, but I soon caught up with my leavings for Treischnitt, leaving much the same kinds of things for Kolberhoff, though to equal disregard, which is to say both Treischnitt and Kolberhoff ignored my existence with the same degree of uninformed aversion, responding to neither my name nor my initials, though of course Kolberhoff ignored me for longer, having outlived Treischnitt, at least until I desisted altogether. Two men, so important in my young life, yet so aloof to me. It hardly bears thinking about, though I have long pondered the chance of any minute differences between what I left Treischnitt and then Kolberhoff, proud famous painters both. Look them up now, meaning in reference books (not calling on them in person), and you will never find them, nor, as it were, in the last glimpse of their dying eyes the last painting they looked at: one of mine. What they did do has slid into the chasm of what they did not do, which has vanished altogether, whereas several violent deformers of mankind's noble face, and the trim honor of its windowboxes, have gone on from generation to generation, Urlschelb and Grenzhabe and Tlöch, to name only a few offenders who vanquished Treischnitt and Kolberhoff, although both Treischnitt and Kolberhoff were the more gifted, lacking as they were in social graces. One day, my face wrapped tight in a huge brown scarf, I accosted Treischnitt and thrust a small coin in his hand, just to see what he would do, but he merely gaped, which Kolberhoff did not do when I pennied him; he only laughed. In the end, all my solicitations came to naught as the opiners who passed judgment on me and my toil happened to be Treischnitt's and Kolberhoff's juniors, crass imitators at the most. Whom did I have to kiss to prosper? In whose fist put coin? Besides, I had not the time to get on with serious work and at the same time conjure up little pastels and quaint greetings for Treischnitt and Kolberhoff. I would have had more success groveling before a statue of Frederick the Great or Charlemagne. It is hard to learn what you need not do in this world, whom you must woo and whom you must spurn. You make choices as best you can and then get thrashed by the heirs of Treischnitt and Kolberhoff, our beloved native land being the one that boasts the most decorations and orders, sashes and stars, almost even a satin gown for yawning. However, without having spun in the periphery of Treischnitt and Kolberhoff, I would never have understood the canker that afflicted their heirs, to whom Treischnitt and Kolberhoff were generous Neanderthals. It was nearly enough to make me want a war to break out, something that would kill me off and so spare both Treischnitt and Kolberhoff the embarrassment of my juvenile attentions, tracking them at a distance when they sometimes went for a walk together puffing on cigars (Treischnitt's a Turkish flavor, Kolberhoff's more a Balkan Sobranie). I have always loathed tobacco, but, following the two of them, I made a small sacrifice, though it seemed as if the two tobacco aromas fused into what two men with stomach trouble might have vented behind them. Did they see me? I doubt it. Treischnitt and Kolberhoff walked together only because no one would accompany either and provide a good quarrel, which was all they walked for, jabbing at the air and wagging an index finger in the direction of their march. An ungenerous person would say I was obsessed with Treischnitt and Kolberhoff, but rather I was a case of highly developed loyalty, knowing, as they say (not Treischnitt and Kolberhoff but everyone else), where my bread might be buttered provided either of these grand old nobodies was willing to hoick the butter from its shelf and ply the butter knife: Must help this promising little chap with his career, not leave the privilege to deadheads. It must have gone like that if Treischnitt and Kolberhoff talked about me at all, lamenting my uncouth ways, my persistence, but recognizing at the same time my classical ardor, for what is classical is what all agree on. It is not a freak thing. There is a social sanction. So you might wonder what those two blockheads Treischnitt and Kolberhoff were arguing about, dyed-in-the-wool classicists that they were. It was not as if rival schools of portraiture, say, were having at each other, Köbel and Steinitz and Probstschule against Klarf, Ulruhst and Delbers, which would have been up-roarious, no, but Kolnsheft having at Döbelzeiss, who as you well know spent their lives at other people's throats. No, there is a way of arguing that celebrates the sun, the trees, the lapping water, and two die-hard opponents can exchange insults above a bridge of natural agreement. Had I had my chance to quarrel or agree with either Trei-schnitt or Kolberhoff, my two art-hounds lolloping on before me by some fifty meters or so, I might have ex-torted from either a recognition that would pay off end-lessly in finer technique to the end of my days. I was de-prived of that if you can be deprived of what you have never had. My own doctrine, of how the watercolors ac-tually tasted as you sipped the mohair bristles to a sharp point, might have joined us in an entirely new school of art: burnt sienna—tea; Naples yellow—baby-dung; alizarin crimson—blood of a dog. What a wide-open world of experiences awaited them at my hands, but it never happened, and on they droned, painting with their eyes; maybe noting a little smell now and then, but quite severed from the world of taste, which was almost like not eating. Treischnitt and Kolberhoff (I would address them

thus jointly like two linked cars in a train) remained con-
joint in their indifference, pseudo-quarreling only to ce-
ment their bond. At my wildest, then, I would do my best
to invade the sleep of one or the other, Treischnitt or Kolberhoff, even when Treischnitt was dreaming about Kolberhoff with candid aversion, or Kolberhoff about Treischnitt with undisguised envy or indeed either dreaming
about the other's dreaming about him. I was in there, in
the gaps, egging them on to further resentments or sun-
nier loathings, wishing to roost in their minds for ever,
nudging this or that flash of dare I say it genius? All imagined, of course, as if I were the proprietor of dreamland,
developing scripts and scenarios for these two malleable
giants to perform amid their snores. Why they never
smoked cigars while napping I never knew, but they
could have, such was their power. Walking behind either
of the two men is one thing, but dreaming along with
them is another, requiring invasive skill, even to the extent of fondling this or that part of their anatomy in order
to give a misleading effect, though I made their most private parts soggy as battered milkwort, just to stimulate
their minds. From sleep with me, they would arise rum-
pled and ill-rested, and I imagined myself as never quite
going away but sojourning under the bed, right beneath
the point at which the mattress creaked most. Truth told,

10

even if you loathe your targets, you eventually come to enjoy something about them, the curve of an earlobe, say, or the tilt of the septum. There they lay, my two hearties, aesthetic men of war, even as I scribbled and scrawled in my mind's eye the masterworks that would join me to them in after-years, not exactly inspiring me, but embodying the impetus of the true artist, whom nothing distracted from his toil. At times, in dreams or out, I would fancy myself mixing pencil shavings into my porridge to crispen it up as well as to make it more artful, or squeezing a little burnt sienna into the mustard (some friends of mine painted in mustard, boot polish, and a white paste for tennis shoes called Blanco, imported from that haven of taste England). All I was trying to do, unlike Treischnitt and Kolberhoff, was to fuse the world of art with that of not-art, easier to say than to do, almost to the point at which you could not tell a postcard from what it depicted. Perhaps to accomplish this one needed satanic help, a Faustian touch denied me at that time, since it was a mode of magic hitherto unknown in the world of visual art. Such prodigies we try for, we doodlers among the pigments and powders, lubricating our brains with linseed or water. In a word, as I would have told both Treischnitt and Kolberhoff, I was trying to force the created into perfect similarity, with nothing extraneous allowed.

11

Hence my leaning toward those two worthies, as distinct from the even more renowned Klötzheide, Funknasch, and Zwölftraum, esteemed because more socially adroit than either of my two Magi. I would one day, I hoped, be even more adroit than they, always tucking my shirt in, never accepting a penny from strangers. You see how I keep looking back, an act about which I have thought a good deal, hour after hour while plucking fibers from the old run-down sofa in my garret, horsehair bursting out at all angles like a beast having a hemorrhage. Put it this way. If you are in your teens, and you keep on looking back on your earlier teens from the vantage of your later teens, then you are more in tune, more closely connected, than if you are looking back at your teens from your fifties, say (if you get that far). It sounds right: the closer you are to what you look back on, the warmer, the keener your recollect will be. I don't believe it. The whole enterprise is one of how articulate you are. People have told me that the closer your idiom is to that of the period you are recalling (nineteen recalling eighteen, say), the more convincing your account is, but only if you have ruled out the refinement and delicacy of a much later speaker, writer, who can muster many more shades and gradations, subtleties and hunts, than the nineteen-year-old. The ultimate caricature of the view I am rejecting is that

12

of the three-year-old infant babbling about being Age
Two. What I am after, given the time, is what someone
called the faint subterfuges of untutored eloquence, as if
the words themselves had understood. The man of fifty,
even with blurred and blighted recall, can make more of
his infancy than the hobgoblin of twenty-one. Not that it
matters: we are lucky when anyone at all gets it right, this
excavation of the heart, supervised by a hurt intellect that
tells itself there has always, all along, been a *Doppelgänger*
dogging his steps, preceding him in all things, treading in
his footprints, seating himself on the warmed-up toilet,
eating off the cleared plate, brushing the already scoured
teeth. It comes to either this or, as I once discovered, ram-
bling about old Vienna, some two hundred old geezers in
a huge hall, all playing cards, waiting for the ax to fall.
Honing their minds of course. A stronger image, that,
than the Jew raving on Saturday, the Christian raving on
Sunday, and who knows how many other religious mani-
acs bellowing their faith above the traffic. As may be obvious, this is a later me telling the tale, not in the least hot
on the heels of the pimply, raucous teenager, which of
course tells you that I survived the years in between,
somehow, yet forever awed by the alter ego I might have
become. I could feel him edging up on me, stealing my
body aroma for his, clipping his toenails on my own foot.

13

Who he was will not bear saying, but perhaps he was only one of dozens sent to plague me as I strove to become somebody worth locking in jail for his outlandish ideas, his reckless thirst for power. In my time I came across theories that helped me to fathom who these other beings, my accompanists, were: Errol von Knechtvold, for instance, who said that our heads were full of voices from pre-history, which was the source of myth, or Joachim Kernsvogler, who said all echoes were prophetic. How impossible, say I, to collect up all the disparate bits of a possible you and make them firm, permanent, under one umbrella. If others help, now with a thrashing, now with a failing grade, it might be managed, but not without consummate pain. Experts are those who have dodged their own questions by blocking the avenue of thought with parboiled clichés. If you have sat at the feet of a wiseacre, or pawed the fly of a genius, you are even more on your own than before; the answer is only in what's impetuous, done without thought but with the whole crescendo of biased atoms behind you. I am bound to lose both Treischnitt and Kolberhoff, my lightning rods, without whom I have no alpha and omega, not that they did not overlap: Treiberhoff and Kolberschnitt, my two whatever other combination appeals. Without either of them to serve as backsight and foresight, I will have to take in the all, *Blick ins Chaos,* as we sometimes say: peer into the mess. A migraine follows, and then you are painting in a chrome-flashing gloom. Better to have them back, hale them back, as zombies, kicked this way and that, than have no inkling of them at all, their faces contorted and wizened, their hands mowing about, their feet splayed. Push them when they will not serve, almost as if you were the one's mother, Frau Treischnitt, the other's spouse, Frau Kolberhoff. Always to either they were little lads, two friendly little lads with roving eyes, changelings to both *Frauen,* twins of a kind like those English poets Browning and Tennyson, who took long walks together without ever speaking. I have always been an admirer of the English way, the only nation that has found a real place in civilized concourse for aloofness, porridge, disdain, snottiness, raspberry jam, and the stiff upper lip (better than a penis in many circumstances). But it was the highly decorated Viennese I had to cope with, wondering why amid so many titles I had none myself (would that come?), though I imagined that all the sumptuous cream cakes I could not afford, but watched being sucked on, were honors I would one day merit and receive with open mouth, tongue poised to taste. All productive of the finest chrome yellow gases, blown away by the corrupt circular breeze, akin to a Wild Western dust devil that never left

the esplanade of the cafés. How do you get on in the art
world? You behave as if it is all over and you predicate all
you do on a *réclame* long past, yet nonetheless there to be
counted on, a launching pad for every wild overture.
Hence your confidence, invented, cast behind you, spon-
soring you without yet having been. These complexities
at first stirred me, but I then took them for granted,
knowing I would sweep all before me as an old soul does,
born wrinkled, but chronically expert in the ways of the
climb. Just be yourself and ask: that was it, simpler than
bowel movement, more direct than the yawn. If only it
were so. Small wonder that, peering through the mesh of
the Treischnitts Herr and Frau and the Kolberhoffs Herr
and Frau, and all the varied combinations of the four held
before my gaze like the muslin we drape hanging beeves
with, I lost track of who I was, as well as of what I was
meant to be, compensating—if you will tolerate such a
word—by overdoing everything, even the muted pencil
touches that completed an acanthus leaf on a frieze. It
might be put thus: Lost amid the world of infinite mis-
chance, he became palely hyperbolical, imagining
grotesque picnics with Frau Treischnitt and Frau Kolberhoff, rubbing steel wool against huge bulges under their
skirts until the blood came and a stench of slaughterhouse
washing arose to pollute the countryside and the suave

16

aromas of champagne and wicker hampers. A violent
child overgrown, you might say. Say it then, I have no in-
hibitions about being damned. The urgent thing, amid a
million tangents, was to cut the first niche in my cliff of
fame, clinching my status with a few well-designed water
colors faintly daubed here and there with Frau and Frau
blood, Treischnitt and Kolberhoff thumbprints, and whatever else lay to hand, always tinting ever so quietly, so
much so that not an examiner would be able to tell the
chromatic tremor in the atmosphere from a tremor in his
eyelid. Auersberg Palace, then, around 1911: meticulous
corners and high fluted goblet shapes, but the people
dwarfed, as befits, none of them asked me for preferential
treatment, and I wanted to convey how many of them it
would take to cram that vacant square: a mere half-dozen
seemed to halt in mid-float, even the one wheeling something, perhaps a barrow or a child's scooter, none of them
appearing to look at the others, scratched in as if on
metal, and enormously humbled by the dominant slab
and the infinitely increasing steps. Here you can count
the chimneys (four) and guess at the minarets. Actually
the figures in the foreground have come from another
age and time, the returning dead, all sloping with a limp I
have arrested with a stroke of my pen. What a lovely studio he must have created this in, its atmosphere velvet and

17

gold moiré, except it has only the merest rug in it that re-
sembles not a rug but the recently removed skin of a
wolfhound, smeary and rank, hurled in a rage across the
biggest smirch on the concrete floor. On this I lie, *repose,*
licking the inside of a wooden can, my tongue already de-
formed into shape by the constant licking of such con-
tainers and my hand weary of holding it skyward for the
final drip. What was it? Beets or broken kohlrabi? Washed
down with water from the peat-smelling pump outside,
where dogs crouch at the snarl. What drops on me from
the ceiling—mauve, slimy, and warm—I have no idea,
but I keep them from my mouth, oh yes you blithe comfortable buggers at the windows of the Auersberg Palace,
watching the most inspired of his rotten generation swig
the slop. Something has to keep body and soul, hand and
imagination, together, even if only the drip from the broken roof above, dropping by the light of a rare candle, its
ration of light about two hours. It is my only palace. In
they go. Who has more right? Perhaps even an embossed
pass issued by the Herr Doktor Professor Burgomaster,
Saint Peter of the Auersberg gate. They part company,
Treischnitt the thin and fairly tall off to the left, tapping at
doors and windows with his umbrella's steel tip (no doubt
touched with curare), dumpy Kolberhoff going to the
right, where he taps on nothing but speeds up his waddle.

They arrive, brood, do their task, followed by huge clang-
ing sounds of reservoirs being emptied, not so much the
gush of pent-up water as the self-willed onrush of a sea.
Oh good, it has all gone, and like two spry little colts Treischnitt and Kolberhoff reappear to get on with the day's
examining or form-filling. No painting here, not by them
or anyone else. Who has followed them into those sultry
doorways, edging in disguised as a raincoat or wraith,
there to carp or plead in some office, not with a painter?
One day I alone will. I hope I will. I have to or I become
a potato scumbler for life, scooping out eyes and stripping
skins. In we go, after them, following, as if this were physically possible, the peppermint aroma of Treischnitt, the
Sobranie of Kolberhoff, I as if a little dog sniffing the
crotches of women. Those paltry figures in the front
courtyard have not moved: scarecrows, symbolizing
something awesome, perhaps an old Greek idea that the
word symbol recalls. Once upon a time, everything was all
of a piece and only symbolism gives us back that halved-
up world, whose main crime is to divide the image from
the things seen. It recalls for me the image of the ship, not
an ocean liner but sizeable, that in bad weather broke
clean in half, the two halves floating off in different directions in the dark and fog. The few survivors, clinging to
wreckage, were delighted, when dawn broke, to find two

19

rescue ships bearing down on them from different quarters, arriving at laudable speed with minimum delay. Imagine their chagrin when the two mercy vessels coming to pick them up turned out to be the two halves, hulks, of the original, the worse for wear, once more coming together, or near enough, of course not making it, but evocative in their proximity of a serener outcome. In some moment of deluded optimism, did the survivors imagine the two halves, bow and stern, would come back together and fuse? Such things happen only in the golden dimension of Greek metaphor, when, say, image and thing join up as they should after eons of severance! But no, neither on the high seas nor in the etymological lexicon, does this kind of reunion happen. The survivors stick it out if they can, longing for yet another boat, or at least to get aboard either remnant and flourish before one or the other of them founders and vanishes. Or even both. Only the Greeks with their consummate sense of the unity of all created things would imagine the reunion of things that, by human fecklessness, had been thrown together ages ago. What a luscious idea, to reunite what has been sundered. I am the healer of ikons, I tell myself even as I shuffle up the steps of the Kohler Adlon, hover in the hallway having inhaled the perfume of the porte cochère, and now peek into the unguarded dining room, actually

helping myself to a menu that has fallen, fluttered, in from
Mars. If you can afford it, a three-shrimp appetizer called
Three Whorls, on a bed of chopped fennel smothered in
tangy mustard, will cost you what two dozen shrimp cost
you in the green market. You pay for the ambience, the
thundering suavity. Of course. It is all in the presentation,
at least before they turf me out, shady loiterer, no credit
given for artistic endowment or noble sentiment. Down
the steps I go, but not before seeing and longing for the
dark green jade table on which the guestbook sits, as marine a green as there has ever been streaked with slashes of
cornered sunlight. On such a table I will one day write
autobiography, spelling out in greater detail all that happened to me in composing this brief entry. As if I had
hope of something's happening to me, something grand.
What does the great Goethe say of such palaces as the
Auersberg? We spend our time building palaces, and
adorning them, when we cannot even dispose of our own
excrement. How this bears on the career of the artist will
emerge: we cannot help having to have the palaces, of
course not. Who wants to say, in spite of all, he has devoted his life and gifts to sewage disposal? It is clear that,
even if you happen to be Treischnitt or Kolberhoff, you
bide your time, postponing the delicious moment until
you are consummately ready, bound to prevail, with no

carping from overfed vests crowned with mayoral watch chains. I pause and pause and pause, ever hoping to improve on the work just finished, knowing I can, I must, I will, but having to sleep on it, dream on it, let it wander unescorted through the labyrinth of my peristalsis and heartbeat. One day the heart almost stops, pulsing in a rapid frenzy in its cage, and you know you have to go, abandon your work to the appraisers in a room full of farts and aphorisms, leaving it behind to the sort that Treischnitt and Kolberhoff are without their actually being Treischnitt and Kolberhoff. Someone will squinny at your life's gift and pull a sour face, saying tell him to wait another ten years. Or, in the tradition of some famous British university, possibly impervious Oxford, the examiners work themselves into a sherry-fed frenzy saying we demand a meeting, we must lay eyes on this genius before he melts or dies. It is called A Congratulatory First, whatever that means. It means you have come in before all others, racehorse style, but have landed in heaven without cantering through the gutter of the hoi polloi. What a pipe dream. What opium. Yet I always shrink from that terminal encounter, even with my Auersberg masterpiece, knowing it will not be a masterpiece, even to Treischnitt and Kolberhoff, within a month of hard endeavor.

Up the ladder I go, on limp rungs. This is why, in some
kind of decorous declension, you never get around to the
coup de grâce, which some not in the know call the *coup de
gras,* knowing you are indefinitely capable of something
better. Thus, at seventeen, you get cold feet, at eighteen
butterflies, at nineteen the shakes, at twenty the cold-lard
belly contortions, at twenty-one—well, let us not paddle
fingers in the tragic vomit of twenty-one, an age at which
both Treischnitt and Kolberhoff were going strong, having not only satisfied the examiners, but piled up the
work, actually selling it to the blind. I have dallied, I con-
fess; I am always dallying, but some piece of my chrysalis
goes through the gates and offers curdled heart's blood to
the synod of judges, hoping for miracles, but expecting
shame. You have to begin somewhere, so say my allies August and Reinhold, but they are more gifted painters than
I, and there comes at that moment an intuition of some
other way of becoming great, of making the angel
Gabriel turn tail, bowing low before a superior tender-
ness. Yet I try, knees knocking, up to the Auersberg, in my
insolence having depicted, *my* fashion, the very building
in which I am to be reviewed, down whose steps I have
been tossed a score of times for loitering, just to catch a
glimpse of winning entries, even a pisshouse scrawl done

23

by one of the elect, even while wetting my trousers, fouling my ragged shirt, reddening my eyes. So it begins, inasmuch as it has not already begun. Who is to know when the tendrils of an event do not grow backwards into the source or the cause, alerting the wise as to what is to come? I had rehearsed this, yearning for a mirror in my hovel, but making do with shadows, addressing chiaroscuro on the wall when the sun came in right, high up, deforming all it touched. I began with the mohair question, which astounded them since they were painters in oils and I, when I was anything, was a water colorist, but they made some joking reference, Treischnitt and Kolberhoff, to people who paint with their fingers and noses, all depending on what social class they came from. They could see I was trying to be polite in the most relevant way, lump of turnip safely secreted in that old punctured balloon I had found floating through the Kölnstrasse, beside my bits of purloined schnitzel and cabbage. Perhaps there was even a morsel of dead starling in there, fatally hinged to the turnip by its wing or the claw of its foot. Emergency rations, these, against a long interview. This was the dreaded *Abschied* interview, so called because it sorted the candidates out, bidding most of them *farewell* before any of their work had come into question. It was a matter of fitness and training, you could tell that from

24

their very demeanor. Strange about the balloon. Though punctured, it kept my victuals fresh, almost good enough to offer them, but I refrained of course. You never know what a refined gentleman is or is not allowed to eat. At certain ages, certain foods—well, enough of that. On it goes, and I swiftly tune in to the right approach, shifting from water colors and mohair to what I thought suitable for the occasion: some talk of turpentine, but which, thanks to nervousness, I kept getting wrong whenever I spoke it, starting with turfentide, turpsentice, and turfind-ict, going as far as serpenthyme and earthentide. They got the general idea, though, mocking me a little, Treischnitt and Kolberhoff, often dreamed about though never at such close quarters as this. There had been no rehearsal of such nearness, not even of such topics as squeezing the tube, Squeezing the Tube, a matter of enormous delicacy: from the top or the bottom, rolling up the bottom to keep the tube neat, or leaving little bulges for later call-up, conferring an additional delight of something over-looked and now commandeered into the final crushing sweep. Out it came, whatever color, crying to be mixed and used, not on the palette but directly on to canvas, I said boldly, to air my knowledge of how they did their work. What of crimps? They did not respond to that, of course, heeding no date or manufacturer, and I quietly abandoned the idea of peeling off the label, thus making all tubes alike, the only means of identifying them being to peer into the bowels through the nozzle. None of that, nor any of my proposed blather about easels, resting the eyes on a color not recently worked in, but Treischnitt with Kolberhoff assenting, told me that, after years of worry, he had learned how best to cover wet oils, by draping a pair of lady's voluminous bloomers over the work. The resulting stains, he confided, Treischnitt, Kolberhoff fussily assenting, were more exciting than anything he'd seen. I agreed, promising to drape knickers over my watercolors in future, taking special note of the taint of stains and wondering at their possibly imaginary source. These were the obiter dicta of successful gentlemen, and I was more than eager to pass muster. What came next, however, now we had all three settled down, and the supplementary questioners—a Grenzhaus and a Plöchnasch, I recall, unknown to me for their art or even their demeanor—had left, having satisfied themselves about the major part of the examination, though not about me. Now the gloves were off. Treischnitt began it as he would, taking a comb, bidding me stand, and quietly combing my lank, dark hair upwards into a lolling tod. I had not washed it in readiness for the interview, not suspecting it would figure among the questions, or the issues, but I knew it was greasy, therefore lank, and would fall in that disastrous dun cable across my right eye, slinking forward over my eyes because I had never cut it off or paid a barber to do it for me. There it stood, collapsed, dangled, a monument to my own sexual mishaps, and Treischnitt groaned, echoed by you know whom, as if I had located Bellini in the wrong century. He's a goner, he sighed. He was a goner when he came in, Kolberhoff said. Now he's doubly useless. Perhaps a little bone-glue, the kind they make from fishheads, would hold it up. Or horses' bones, crooned Treischnitt. He has no future if his hair won't stand to attention when combed. Up, boy, he shouted, as if bracing an animal for an endurance test, trying once again, but all fell down from the preposterous height he had raised it to, quite a length when unsettled from its resting place, with all the dandruff, like a shower of corpseflakes from the nearby Ganges of my face, floating up and then to their dismay settling on the table. Look at that, said Treischnitt, who always spoke first, being older, and Kolberhoff was used to this. *He sheds.* Yes, I shedded. You shed, Kolberhoff added. I do, I told him. I should never shed. No, don't ever again shed on my desk. I will never again shed on your desk, I said, or the desk of the Honorable Doktor von—Enough of that groveling scheiss, either Treischnitt or Kolberhoff said (it was the

27

former, I deduced, as one could). That part of the test was over, thank God, and I had spent nights boning up on perspective and such crap. Was not *pointillisme* in the air? It got worse when they opened my fly without probing further, to discomfit me as I stood there, and then asked me to remove my mud-caked boots. My work, I began, but they silenced me, indicating that the most serious part of the interview was already under way, pounding me with questions I had never dreamed of. How much horsehair was there in canvas? In Prussian blue, they asked in unison like a fugitive couple from operetta, heavily im-plying yes. I recoiled, brushing frantically at my quiff, which had fallen forward to bisect my forehead, thanks to their upward-combing endeavors. Now I was truly an unkempt candidate. On it went, from impossible to gro-tesque, if that is the right order in deterioration, when things are really going to pot or to hell. Iron filings in lamp black? I had heard nothing like this. Where was my beloved work, cherished over so many years and brought here by hand in sackcloth with a mouth full of ashes? Next, we discussed the use of various cheeses in priming a canvas, tea leaves in linseed oil (and the visual spatter they made), after which we paused, as if we had accom-plished something profound. Not far away, two female voices raised in shrill dissent nagged at our attention (I proud to use the plural, fusing my attention with theirs, but it was true). Was I passing? Had I failed? Was I going to be a painter after all? Or just a victim? If this last, I was going to turn a few of them into victims of my own, quizzing them in my fifties and sixties until they could stand it no longer. But no, it was lunchtime, or the hour of the feedbag. One never quite knew what realm of being was going to appeal to them next and dominate their current of behavior. Animal, vegetable, or mineral. Lunch was brought, but first two identical sashes, the Danube Silk, which Treischnitt had won eleven times, Kolberhoff only ten (a source of much debate in the coffeehouses). We ate normally enough, breaking our black bread into tiny divots and pecking at sausage. We might have been sparrows or starlings even. I fished for and found my bit of turnip, which they refused with disgust, then a few crumbs they waved away. I would even eat the balloon, choking myself to death to please them, but they motioned otherwise, spurning my death throes and warning me to ready myself for the next phase, the even more dreaded *Wilkommen* or Welcome test, which had to do, so went the rumor, with one's actual work. Had I then passed the preceding interrogations? I must have. I was so overjoyed I choked on my turnip, which I had gnashed at in mingled relief and shame. Now, fuelled up, they were

ready for me. Look at this balls, Treischnitt was saying as
the waiter paraded in with my Auersberg horizontal on a
tray and a leek straddling it, he can't draw. His people are
stalks of celery. Is there no accuracy left in the world? I do
declare, Kohoff, if one took the trouble to measure up this
stuff, it wouldn't pan out. Clearly he has never sighted using his finger. He has no regard for the loveliness of human anatomy. What shall we do with him? I began to
shake and hiccup. The faint subterfuges of something or
other came upon me and left me empty. I was failing at
this very moment. Emboldened by whatever force, I cried
out, You haven't even looked, you turkeys. He has spirit,
Treischnitt said, shall we let him off? One day, you can see
it, he will achieve a position of superb power, and we shall
be proud to have failed him. Look at the other work, I
hissed. They did. They said the same. I took mustard and
added a few drastic mustaches to the stonework of my
Auersberg, shocking them with my apparent abandon
and openness of mind. Ah, said Treischnitt, now he's a
bloody Norwegian, just look at him. There's hope yet, old
boy. They lit cigars as catalysts to serious thought, and
looked again at my poor Auersberg. He's certainly added
something, Treischnitt observed, eyeing my brown and
yellow mottled sweeps, *sans brosse.* Depraved indifference

to human life? Kolberhoff sighed and said no, it was a misdemeanor, as if citing a manual of jurisprudence. There were no laws in those times about what a painter might or might not read, especially one with eleven or ten Danube sashes for—what the hell did they give those sashes for? I was sighing, but they were not buying. He could be a carter, I heard. Or a hotel porter. A toilet cleaner has a good future, as the great Goethe once said, spurning the job himself, except in his work. Treischnitt and Kolberhoff then spoke as one: No. Come back in six months to repeat the entire examination. Since you have failed in one part, the parts in which you passed have also become failures. This is known in the profession as the Leviticus Spillover, a deadly formula originating in the Ukraine. No appointment, good sir. Just keep stopping by to ask if we are in. I was ushered out, my mustard Auersberg under my arm, my face a cashiered white, my step unsteady. However, before you go, they had said, we would like to nominate you for one of the Fisher King Fellowships, which brings you a garret, a regular supply of black bread and kipper paste for one year, during which you are to create your best work. You eat the same thing every day, receive no money, but live rent-free, the entire award based on *chutzpah*. In all probability you have no gift, but a certain amount of initiative, in which we choose to invest just to see what comes of it. All will depend, mein Herr, on how you perform with us on your next visit, which might be timed with Herr Kolberhoff's receipt of an eleventh Danube Sash for—well, it is universally known what he gets awards for. So keep this in mind. You could be living off the fat of the land in no time at all, the kipper of it anyway. Don't fret. All is well. You will have to reconcile your goals with your gifts, good sir. Stop following us. Do not send any more postcards or leave vegetables on either stoop. We do not need your charity or your obsequious attention. Can you not see we are grand old men such as they do not make any more? We are not Norwegian crazies. Nor German fanatics. Remember the country's enormous contribution to world culture, indeed to Treischnitt and Kolberhoff, who now record you in the examination book as having appeared here and done your duty. We do not need you, but one day you may need us when you have reached toilet level. See you in the basement, sir, and be busy. Out I fell. I had suddenly remembered that Vienna, of all cities, was the one with the most photographers' studios. The Viennese more than anyone wanted to record and look at one another, at themselves, capturing every available moment, even boxers with a broken jaw wired together but sucking up soup, or somebody not necessarily a clown being fired out of a cannon pointed at Poland. Or mundaner things: medals, sashes, velvet robes, floppy hats, *regalia* of all kinds, flowers made from paper, artists at work copying the work of their undistinguished forebears. Even someone being sarcastic to a pregnant woman. Vienna loved to watch Vienna and did not need the rest of Austria, certainly not Europe, able to find in the mirror all that mattered in your 70 x 365 days on earth. Or in a lovely blowup, huge from the enlarger's hands. Oh, one day, would I too have photogravure of the epauletted shoulder, the chained waistcoat, the emblazoned arm, the beribboned and bemedalled chest, the heartspoon hidden by a huge gong that glinted and flashed? Would I, looking at my own image, see only grandeur, the humble soul transformed into the scion of epic moment? How did one make a start? By bending the knee to Treischnitt and Kolberhoff, calling them my lord and your worship, herr doktor von and illustrious sire. They, who had received, knew how to give, surely.

Here I come, slinking brickward

HERE I COME, SLINKING BRICKWARD in the hour of lavender, to what I call my sentry box, a niche in a wall really, opposite a restaurant called Terza Rima. Brick above me, to one side decrepit stone, behind me ironwork of indeterminate design as of a garden gate mangled. It is where I observe the evening comings and goings of those who can afford Terza Rima (here too a three-shrimp appetizer for the price of several oxen). I leave my hovel, wondering why, in a place so scruffy, there is the continual smell of new paint, which must well up from some channel in the building, and quite apart from what I am told is my own characteristic body odor: engine smoke, as in railroad, somewhat sulfurous and sooty. Here I lurk, a born lurkster, hoping perhaps to spot Treischnitt and Kolberhoff arriving to spend their ill-gotten pelf, little pondering the fate of those living on the fringe, unable to eat friendship, doomed to fill the belly with water from the local pump, to wash and

shave in the same place. They have, as it were, gone beyond, confining themselves to a studio of well-lit north-
ern aspect, in which the light seems no longer a priceless
gift from an uncaring Creator. Myself, I paint in the semi-
darkness, which is no doubt what they picked up in my
Auersberg and disliked so much, the lack of light falling
on the people's heads, that commonplace benison. Carriages arrive, honking autos, with money striding out of
them on the prowl for three-shrimp appetizer, bitter
apéritif, creamy desserts from which oozes the white
worm of luxury. The lurkster inhales their perfume, their
cologne, their leather and silk, wishing he had not at-
tended that grisly interview with Treischnitt and Kolberhoff, who after all were not the personages billed as in
charge. Somehow, they shuffled themselves into position
merely to "get" me, relinquishing their chairs as soon as I
vanished. Surely their offered carrot of a Fisher King Fellowship was bogus, a final taunt, retaliation for my
hounding them; but you never know, the whole thing
might have been accidental, and, as ever, I am trying to
make sense of something that makes none but is merely
what happened next. What Happened Next, of which the
world is full, poorly as we accommodate ourselves to it.
Should the pair of them arrive, Treischnitt and Kolberhoff, I would love to overhear them actually praising my

Auersberg, venting the real truth, relieved to admit at last, to each other, the superiority of my work, the legacy from so and so that I have at last fulfilled. Yes, you know, the poor wretch really has something. Awkward lumbering, maladroit, true, but he really has the real thing. Every mother has one, but this one's a nascent genius. No shunting him off to architecture, no fear; he belongs in the atelier of time, apple of the Academy's eye. Well, gentlemen, I am still waiting, and when I barge out of hiding, blistering the night air with my distress, it is as a commissionaire in a topcoat far too big for him, with red and gold epaulets, a fancy hat smothered in festive braid, feet encased in stenchy boots, nose a-run, eyes teeming, hands raw from fending off baggage, my back sore from bowing, my undergarments drenched from standing in the rain all day in the hope of a small coin or two from those over whom I hold an umbrella big as Portugal and just as dry. Beyond such an appointment, at which I huff and puff, ever on the trot, there is only that chore in the basement, to which I am bound eventually to be assigned: toilet man, accustomed to the flush and flatus of an entire civilization. It has not come yet, but soon it will. Commissionaires are ten a penny, are they not? I can almost imagine Treischnitt and Kolberhoff doing my job for me, a double act, but for now, *qua* painter, I retreat into the

39

shadows again, into my so-called sentry box, determined
not to torture myself with dreams of what's to come
There is doom, and there are the little dooms in between:
the pre-dooms, about which it is better not to think. Yet
how many of us, having no political party to succor us,
torment ourselves with the pre-dooms, afraid to envision
the final one, as it were rehearsing the ultimate charade,
our insignia an empty plate crossed with a rat skull. The
thousands of us who gather in the dusk, out of sight, our
hopes as loud as the twitterings of bats, we stand and pray
for something nobler to end with, having been be-
smirched by the Treischnitts and Kolberhoffs in this or
that miserable calling, yet through sheer persistence attuned to the sidechatter of disembarking fat cats who de-
part heavier by several kilos of gravy, cream, steak, kidney,
shrimp and lard. A mere sampling would suit us, get us
through the night, even to inhale their burps, cognac
breath on gravy breath, what a feast, my masters, too rich
a diet for the lungs of the likes of us. We'd burp it back,
would we not? It's what happens when the empty stomach beholds the full one, and the extra fat wobbling on
their ladies' behinds. Just think of all the wet silk trapped
in between. I linger on, recognizing not a soul: no artists
certainly. I would be better loitering at some café mis-

named Des Artistes, at which non-artists search in vain for real artists, who can never afford such dumps. By and large we do not make money. We wince and shrivel, carp and blame, but we do muck our hands with oil and turps, filling in the lonely gaps beneath the nails, wondering how much more we can abide. Few come to get us, though we all believe in rescue by millionaire. Was there not once, is there not to come, a regiment named the Artist's Rifles, perhaps just formed from among the malcontents of London's studios? Against whom? Is it just a bunch of painters eager to kill somebody? I would join if I only knew how. If not them, then the Painters' Brigade, a lordly title to be sure, a brigade of smotherers who wangle their way at night like cat burglars into the homes of the idle rich and there suffocate them with all the oily rags of yesteryear, much as we would if we worked on locomotives all the day. Simply, the oils smell differently. It is a different division of a world order. Visibly, I live in my imagination, hammering away at what is not quite real, but having little else beyond Treischnitt and Kolberhoff to keep me going, and my private vision of the Auersberg. You have to have something to hold to, even if only the cap of the milk bottle, within it a flap you push down so as to reach the contents. We are like that, delivered to the

41

doorstep, the stoop, with a little round cap in the center of which there's a smaller cap to shove down, giving access to our inflamed insides. Prod through the cream at the top and get your finger into the milk of human cream. That does it. I am through with metaphor, banned in the Artists' Rifles and replaced by bullets named for dead painters. Shoot someone with a Da Vinci, someone else with a Hals. Never mind who, just note the name and shoot. This is how all great revolutions begin, with a bitter man in a doorway, empty and cold, his features graced by a current of lavender light from high above, his eyes gloom-adapted, his life's work rolled up into a cylinder in a nameless attic to which not even mice have climbed. I exaggerate. It would be poetic justice if Treischnitt and Kolberhoff were to arrive now, disgorging themselves from an ornate carriage, both got up in commissionaire uniforms, the tailor by royal appointment to the Academy. These men do not so much control Art, they *are* Art. It makes you sick to think of it. Time to move to a different doorway before the police lay hands on me, huffily saying Time now, good fellow, to darken some other spot. You'll need help from an unexpected quarter now, which they say as "Yewl need elp from ha Diffrunt kwor-a." What kind of lingo is that? I have been moved on much more than I have ever moved myself, easily (to put it in vivid terms) all the way from Vienna to Istanbul, rather than

from Istanbul to Ankara. And on foot too. Imagine that.
The shoe leather becomes the merest abstraction, so thin
and translucent you can read newspaper through the soles
provided you tread on it first. We do not so much walk on
rugs as grace them with our sole-prints, becoming experts in texture (Persian, Turkish, et cetera), able to tell
blindfold which rugs are worn, and by whom, and which
are not. Sidewalks scar us and roads make us bleed, we the
sensitive contingent placed on the planet to bother it
while it shields itself from the accumulated sadness of col-
lapsing civilization ripe for a dunt. Shall we be part of
that? Bet your pfennig we will, there being little else to do
other than endorsing checks and visiting bank managers
about the rate of compound interest. Treischnitt and Kolberhoff suddenly arrive, as if summoned up by some in-
cantation, not this, and disappear into Terza Rima like two
airships in dalmatics. One of them is gaunt and narrow,
Treischnitt, but he seems to have fattened up for this out-
ing. Forever talking about me, and eager to sit down
troughing while doing so, they leave behind them like
shreds of bird feather the usual tributes, and I almost bow,
imagining the praise they muster, too shy in their heart of
hearts to say it to my face. So do we all die, trying to better ourselves, trying to cheer ourselves up, not as if Treischnitt and Kolberhoff, two rampant mediocrities, ruled
the world, but as if Treischnitt and Kolberhoff *were* the

43

world, that foul maze of people who never do their jobs
or respond or really work, but miscellaneously get by because they trust one another, all being much the same,
even when they drop dead. The stink is much the same,
the plug in the backside, to stave off the avalanche that so
worried the great Goethe, the same for all. We are only
bags of it in different places with varying labels. If I said all
this out loud, I'd be in real trouble, beating at the bars to
get out in time for my ninetieth birthday, one last look at
Treischnitt and Kolberhoff, choking on butter cream
torte, ever regnant, the semi-kings, the lickers of all private ice creams. Away I shuffle, envying anyone his bicycle, yet determined to wait it out. I no sooner moved than
I wished I had stayed put.In their full glory appeared the
little outdoor tables, sheathed in white cloths, over which
sippers rather than diners huddled as if over altars, their
voices for the most part hushed, their gestures curbed.
There was something mysterious about this hour, spring
or fall, I can rarely tell which, and I wished I were part of
the perpetual ongoing confab that ruled the world, knew
of all the crannies and intervals, the hidey-holes and the
secret bank accounts. I would have behaved myself, back
ramrod stiff, forelock combed back and moored with
lemon curd, eyes bathed to leech out the red. So I stepped
back, thinking this could go on for a lifetime without

anyone noticing me or telling me, in the mode of the place, to get a move on. Perhaps if they saw me at all they took me for a statue, even a virgin in her shawl, or a saint about to be boiled in oil. I was there, but in a sense I was not, I was only Treischnitt's and Kolberhoff's solitary retainer, watching their spears and arrows for them until they resumed the hunt for greatness. What if I sat down without bidding a waiter to seat me, omitting the customary tip that went with the favor, even before you have begun ordering. The logic of life in that place was something like this: I am breathing, so here's a tip for you, thank you very much. Keep me alive. I suddenly wanted to get back to my wooden fork, the holed tablecloth (ravaged linoleum), the wobbly chair, the little stenchy larder that held a breadbin and a cheese cage—as if the cut would get up and walk away propelled, or is it impelled, by its own maggots. I needed no music, no apéritif, no company, beyond Treischnitt and Kolberhoff, nothing on the walls save any one of my aborted works of art. Nor much light, even though I saved the candle's drippings and rolled a tiny offspring cored by a single hair. It never worked, the delirious idea of the potent miniature held sway in my brain as something to patent and one day make me a fortune. Hours I had spent in there, drawing almost in the dark, feeling my way through cornices and

45

pediments, sometimes using charcoal I would accidentally rub away with my torn sleeve, which meant I never saw what I had drawn, just a flurry of lines and smoke as if a locomotive had passed nearby. If this was Hovel Number One, would Two be worse? If so, what must I rehearse for? Swat all flies and stamp all beetles until I have a dark brown paste to make my umbers with, smearing the mixture in place with my thumb to give an effect of spurious stucco. That would be the day, when I invented a new technique, such as scumbling, and my name would appear in the ABZ of Art, next to the man who invented *pointillisme* or *tachisme.* Such dreams. I have not mentioned the goddesses, dangerous and sublime, who arrive at almost any hour, at a safe distance looking almost marble or wooden, but intently fixed upon the enormous slash in their anatomy, the badge of their duty and perspective in life. They always have this in mind, whatever else they seem to attend to. I keep them ethereal or I would never get anything done, for their demands are gross once begun, and art, as I know it, has no time for the imperium of the gash, is an altogether different zone of demand and privilege, demanding of you no less than the goddesses the energy of your entire life. Treischnitt and Kolberhoff, the Treischnitts and the Kolberhoffs know this of course, whatever pretensions they have to pipesmoking at the domestic hearth, ignoring the primal call to go beyond the brown-pink lips at the rim of that cavity-factory. Such delving must be for others who ignore the call of Apollo, and they must risk the imputation to them of inhuman motives. One semi-swoons of course in the perfumed aura left behind them by these temptresses, whose single-mindedness matches my own. No man can say he has not come close to losing his divine spark in those eyes, in the folds of flesh they amble about to flaunt, but the most dedicated of us have to keep our mind intact and push our energy into the drab arena of the canvas, the thick paper of ravishing texture. This is where any Stefanie ends up, of course, adored but physically shunted away, although conserved in the mind as an angelic figure on a festive landing in the act of welcoming an evening's friends, the exquisite hostess, to whom countless love poems have been addressed, lauding her as a damsel of high rank, clad in a dark blue overflowing robe of purest velvet, and, when not on the landing, astride a white palfrey of sheerest delicacy, riding over flower-strewn meadows never trampled before, her loose tresses cascading over her shoulders like a golden flood, above her the bright, keen sky of spring capping a scene of radiant happiness. At such a distance, she is never torrid, although thinking of her evokes Wagnerian moments that are. One honors and disobeys, couching one's amazement in the gentlest figures, knowing this is the bait in the trap, and our entire populated planet the clue to our failure to resist. Besides, if you have to keep abreast of the Treischnitts and Kolberhoffs, ever on the qui vive those two industrious gentlemen, you are too weak for anything else. It is not keeping up with the Joneses, ever reminded of Miss Jones and Mrs. Jones, as my adored British say, but dragging after Treischnitt and Kolberhoff in their incessant forays and endeavors, never if you can help it getting left behind. Have your Rubens cake, but do not eat it except during some elated picnic of the mind, preferably to the tunes of *Rienzi*. In the mind's eye some visual echo of Makart while, with some male friend, a Kubizek, you clamber up the Freinberg, there to contemplate the august town lying beneath, and surrender to the tide of images that mounts inside, purges you, and will not leave you be until it has washed you clean with a vision of the future in which you will not lead, of course, though your works will flank the triumphal archway through which the nation marches to glory. Inspired by art, an entire people would forget its pain and mishaps: not exactly the world envisioned by Treischnitt and Kolberhoff, whose feet of clay

48

hold them back, but akin, simply because they have had more time in which to amass sublime images for which as they calculate they will never be forgotten. It is hard, in recounting this, not to think it is happening all over again, thriving in the present and future tenses, instead of being treasured in retrospect as what actually happened before all else, but I dangle between enthusiastic recall and transport back into the moment, all subsequent life erased, only those austere magical moments remaining. Who can be strong enough not to slip back into his youthful ecstasies, glorying in a picture that has no frame but sucks him in for the most delicious amnesia of all? It was like that before I ever went near Vienna, when I was dazzled and captivated as by a collection of fine diamonds, by the Ringstrasse, splendid as Aladdin's Cave, museum upon museum, in which it was possible to imagine my own work installed in the permanent collection. In that trance of overpowering opera and sublime visual visitation, I knew I had the spiritual wherewithal, even if not the financial, but a crescendo awaited me, could I but tear myself away from places almost as beloved, just as my own father had done many years before, resolved to make something of himself as he strode out with scarcely a backward glance. The power to sever, or, if not quite that, to freeze and annul the parts of one's being that hold one back, that is the discipline of the upward climber whom I also call far-ward, the yearner emancipated from his own froth and gearing himself for the kind of applause most men only dream of. For *them* the arid formulas of schooling, the chapter and verse of a so-called education. My love was the flux, ricochet from God's own indecisiveness, that called out to us to make what we could of this turmoil; to the strongest the prize! Batten on to those who have won and suck their secret from them as during one of those sustained childhood kisses, usually an arm, when you kiss and then suck and suck until the whole area reddens and flecks of blood appear. The blood-kiss we urchins dubbed it, it left a speckle behind it, perhaps a bruise, but the recipient knew she had been honored and savored. So, I would blood-kiss Treischnitt and Kolberhoff, swiftly gathering up the vital names from gossip and discarded newspapers, aiming myself like a hawk until the chivalrous day I was taken in, "made of their company," and encouraged to continue without having to go through any more of the twizzles that guaranteed the future of the imagination and the heart, all childhood romance left behind me as I towered without teetering, with nary a swagger, even strolling two paces behind Treischnitt and Kolberhoff, inhaling the blood aroma from their exhaled smoke as the wind seized it and elaborated

50

it this way and that, knowing I had arrived. Once you have arrived, you endure, you do not always need to work at it, any more than a train, having chugged into Vienna, has to labor further, not even to disgorge. To accomplish this goal, I made my sacrifices, as who does not, but not such as leave a scar, leaving Mama, Mama alive, Mama dead, but the young artist or the young grenadier has to harden himself at some point, even if it takes him a year and a half to condition himself to the stress of leaving. *They* will not go away from *you,* you go away from them. This doctrine, implanted by who knew whom, ultimately enabled me to break away Vienna-ward, where the enviable baubles lay with blank nameplates on their sides. So I Treischnitted and Kolberhoffed, as I said, to my heart's delight, inhaling energy from the very city, until I became the new Treischnitt/Kolberhoff, talk of the town, wearing the face of glory as calmly as I did sunlight, aping no one, obliging my hosts by being there: what I longed to think of myself, the young man who, striking out on his own, with only his genius to declare, had actually made it, atop the Reinberg once again. The next thing I did was to pretend to be a civilized-looking sipper at a table, oddly crouching there with a westward view to catch sight of the green flash as it is called, when the sun dips below the horizon and the eye's favorite color crackles triumphantly through as all the other colors give up the ghost. I was a poor imitation, very soon ushered on and away, but I had seen the flash and took it home with me, wondering if I should implant it in some work of mine just to test the mind of the viewer. What had Treischnitt or Kolberhoff said about my Auersberg? Consider the foreground in its own right and ask yourself if the figures bear nobly enough their representative role? Some old bunch of rhubarb like that. I did, I isolated them, at the back of my mind the old medical school canard that said if you are not gifted enough to be a doctor, then become a dentist. In my version, sotto voce, it became if you are not a good enough artist, then become an architect. A fine scandal, that. Well, my figures did look scraggy, apart from the one woman on the left, the others perhaps appealing for help, even the two engaged in pulling-pushing the gurney on which I saw at least two barrels not prevented from rolling about. The whole crew had a windblown look, temporary and torn, perhaps merely a hint of our precarious fate in this world, perhaps an index to my lack of interest, then anyway, in the texture of people's being, as the jargon of the schools puts it. You have to know what you are getting into as the actress said to the bishop. Perhaps I should then, so Treischnitt and Kolberhoff, remove the foreground from the painting and treat it as a theme in its

own right, instead of leaving it straggly and scraggy, re-
conceiving it as an esplanade crammed with diners and
sippers all intent on seeing the green flash, craning and
stretching toward the west, but for what who knew? All
minimal action (Treischnitt, Kolberhoff) designed to get
the viewer wondering and thus involved at the level of
fervent interest, rather more than that of an accumulator
battery joined to a front-door lamp. Who can that be at
the door? The lamp does not care. I could see the bowler
hats and gaping corsages of it all, the tiny wind among the
mustaches and spit-curls, but for the life of me I could not
see the commercialization of that plaza as worth doing. I
wanted it empty, almost neglected, to indicate the pomp
of the place behind it. But Treischnitt and Kolberhoff had
said in different ways, with different hurrumphs, the palace and the plaza before it were both dead, vacant, as appealing to a potential buyer as the stone floor of an abat-
toir or the suet of an eviscerated beast hung up by its rear
knees to drain. Was I going to modify it or not? Scribbling
did not help. It would have to be a new work entirely, not
a revamped one, I thought, neither Treischnitted nor Kolberhoffed, my masters, whatever pain it put the potential
buyer to. My own was just that. What it all came to eventually, as might have been expected, was Treischnitt and
Kolberhoff tramping around in the plaza in front of the

53

The Dry Danube

Auersberg, complaining about the surface to be walked on, not smooth enough, the way the wind roared in and spun around, the way the area included so many vantage points that gave a poor view of the building's symmetry, as if the damned place had designed itself. But thus was only their way of being self-important, with ever a misgiving about something of no interest to them. All they wanted to do was be self-important vis-à-vis the likes of me, the aspirant, the nebbish, the greenhorn, lecturing him about, oh, what were the words they used? Contrast, parallel, even demeanor and style. Imagine anyone correcting the demeanor of a building! Nor was I architect enough to care, but they were certainly animating the empty area in front, and that I supposed was their main point, as if four-handedly they had introduced the Renaissance into the regions of the philistine Huns. All balls, that, but it's what those in power do to you when you are in the silly posture of *applying,* as if you don't know anything, can't learn anything, own no books and have not even a set-square to your name. On they tromp like elephants inspecting a burial ground (yours), and lay down the law with fierce tedium, as sure of themselves as those wardens of San Quentin, that American hell-hole, who had all inmates photographed with a mirror so as to save money by doing front and profile all in one. Some Aus-

54

trians know their stuff. Thank God I have Treischnitt and Kolberhoff as whipping boys, popping in to steel me when I least expect it. I would prefer Treischnitt if he were more like Kolberhoff, and Kolberhoff if he were more like Treischnitt, who says with a note of hysterical frenzy: Well at least you didn't cram the foreground with rabble, my lad, you show a certain political sense. This was more Kolberhoff than Treischnitt, but Treischnitt got in first, he the intellectual snob, Kolberhoff the social one. I have nothing to say to them. They irk me even at their most ingratiating. Treischnitt at the gallop is almost worse than Treischnitt backed up by Klaus, Odel, and Pfintner, none of whom support Kolberhoff, who counts on five toadies, as he once said to me, not to Treischnitt his crony: Fnenck, von Traub, von Eschpitz, Dünckner, and Klemp. How they keep them straight I do not know. Does either of them sometimes need the other's henchmen? Are there no henchwomen? Is there no one there to speak up for the dregs, the rotters, the people who have no hope, what used to be called the proletariat of the society? The ones who provided the milk and did the suckling—was that it? Let them, so say Treischnitt and Kolberhoff, drink piss, let them trough on shit like dogs, we have to keep society in strict order, such as clearing the foreground of yours truly's palace drawing. Despicable vacancy, Get some thinkers. So Herr Treischnitt. Bring on some carriages, my boy. So Herr Kolberhoff. Who wound these men up? Might they be fused together by lightning? Great God in heaven, says Kolberhoff, in his cups, We know what this working-class hyena will draw whenever he gets chance, he will empty the scene of the aristocracy, it's as plain as day, only to be corrected by Treischnitt, as often when addressing Kolberhoff his junior, It is not the aristos he wants out of here, it's the smartie-pants, they upset him because they think all the time and he is accustomed to living among polar bears. Ice-bears, Kolberhoff says, I call them ice-bears, as distinct from bugbears and Russian bears, put him in a pit and prod him with pointed staves. Stop indulging him, Treischnitt, but Treischnitt is having none of that, he is top dog after all, he says. A pox on him, we shouldn't be dealing with the likes of him, it's only a matter of a stipend neither of us needs. I don't need it. Neither do you. No, I don't, Kolberhoff admits. We ought to be off in the Alps picking flowers and greasing our wives' buttocks with pigfat for the grand onslaught up there in the thin air. Well, says Treischnitt, I'll be buggered. No you won't, says Kolberhoff, but *they* will, if I have anything to do with it, while this tripehound of an aspirant is drawing the palaces of his betters and who knows what filthy corners of the society he comes from and should return to. There are spaces for gentlemen, but none for ragamuffins. Just so, Kolberhoff, says Treischnitt, who often tells Kolberhoff to stuff his mouth but not on this day of days after the judging, was it not, when they are both quite knackered. Now they are talking, I imagine, about how, I imagine, I draw. Imagine that. He seizes the pencil, says Kolberhoff, talking first as he often likes to, Treischnitt's wit being a bit sharper, and chews on it with his brown teeth, wondering what the fuck to depict, which he then does with all kinds of correct angles as if proving Pythagoras. He is all of that, so Treischnitt goes on: Not knowing in whose head all these bloody angles are. He peruses the ground: Kolberhoff. His ground: Treischnitt. Well, fuck his ground: Kolberhoff. He copies: Treischnitt. He copies other draftsmen: Kolberhoff. Lord I want to throw up, Treischnitt says, he wants to be an artist, He Wants To Be An Artist. Now, what is the Greek for that disease. Balls to the Greeks, Kolberhoff says, derivative megalomania I call it. He shuts up. I hear them and want to kill them, these pansy toadies with their balls in their top pockets. Where have they come from? What lousy country estate threw them out? Fat stuffed Austrian pigeons I'd like to roast on a spit, polite to my face, ravaging monsters behind my back. Call me *he,* they do, I have a nobody for a face. My day will come, but it will have a black border printed around it by the coroner, and all the time the heirs of Treischnitt and Kolberhoff are building a newer trousers press to torture me with: pants by Herr Procrustes. Give up the profession of graphite or take the water torture upside down. Who can be a genius in such circumstances? Only a deadhead would prevail, eyes closed. One of my early mistakes, I realized, had been to gamble all on one drawing, masterstroke or not, when perhaps Treischnitt and Kolberhoff wanted the gamut, all of my moods and ploys in one portfolio: the full man, with not a quirk omitted. So I began to work on another scene from old Vienna, not heirloom palace this time, but a nostalgia-thick corner, knowing this would jerk the tear strings. In addition, I tried to keep better track of their movements, Treischnitt and Kolberhoff, which included the dentist and the colonic irrigation clinic, the artist's provision store (they kept buying although they no longer seemed to paint). Their new habit, unless I had previously been unobservant to a severe degree, was to go about apart, or perhaps fifty meters away from one another, in the park or at the coffeehouse, which was bewildering: anyone habituated to Treischnitt-Kolberhoff watching would at once conclude the other was in the offing when he saw only Treischnitt or Kolberhoff, which meant that he would assume the other was close when in fact he might have been far away. Worse, in seeking the other, you might lose the one you already had, so there was an ever-widening gulf for the eye to accommodate, a vast area to scour even if only for Treischnittiana or Kolberhoffiana—discarded wrappers, bits of tobacco fallen at the smolder and unreclaimed, left to burn on neglected and unsavored. It was a hard, unrewarding time during which I might have popped the question about this or that: how many drawings/paintings to submit next time, whether to tear everything in half and show only the backgrounds or the foregrounds, whether or not if finances ran to such devious extravagance I should sprinkle the right tobacco over the surface, not a lot but an identifiable sprinkling that clung to a thin smear of flour-and-water glue made in the chipped enamel bowl I reserved for all my ablutions. So much entered into the next phase that I wished many a time for a conference with either of them or both, just to air my professional worries and, as it were, steal a march on the market. No such luck. No doubt Treischnitt and Kolberhoff were going about in disguise, in monocles (what did you call two monocles worn at the same time?), huge fur coats, clown rouge and Pagliaccio paste. It was no use asking. Nobody in my acquaintance would believe that in a serious profession such people existed, never doing their jobs, denying they ever

59

had such jobs, certainly claiming they had no dealings with such as me (how many of me were there in Vienna, scuttling like lizards in between the feet of the great as they thundered about in spats?). Visiting their office was a waste of time: no nameplates, no plates below protected glass, no directions painted on the walls, and no unique after-bouquet in the toilets, that ultimate spoor. I knew the aroma of their afterbirths, so to speak, but no amount of covert sniffing gave me any clue. The two most important men in Vienna had done a bunk, which to anyone in the know meant only that they were doing their work in the usual manner of high-placed, high-ranking eccentrics, to whom work was the merest bagatelle, subject daily to impromptu metamorphoses I called camouflage. They were bound to be somewhere, of course, but I soon ceased looking for two men together and began scrutinizing groups of three or four, even five or six (ideal hiding, this), but with no luck. Of course, they should have moved, both Treischnitt and Kolberhoff, into my own building to hide right in front of me; unable to believe my own eyes, I would have discounted the evidence of *all* my senses. But that feeble assemblage of bricks and mortar, mainly chips and fungus, hardly qualified as a building anyway, so it was no use expecting miracles. I went on looking, considered stealing someone's dog and training it

60

to find them, but no dog appealed. Can you believe that in the whole of Vienna I could not find a dog worth stealing? Why, I wondered, were people appointed to jobs they would never do? Answer came that they got those jobs because they did not need them. Such was the animating principle of most communities. Hence the presence of an enormous rump or leftover, these being the qualified that nobody needed: people with degrees, lifelong experience, a real gift for the job and commitment to it. Feckless amateurs ruled the roost, so was this why many of us decided Vienna was ready for a fall? Other cities behaved in just the same way, the key to the whole maneuver being that the city didn't want to be caught out doing anything obvious. You could tell how advanced a city was from the hordes of frustrated people marching about in search of such and such a person supposedly doing a job—sanitary inspector, maître d', plumber, bricklayer, literary critic, house painter—all in vain. All you ever found was the literary critic, say, with a trowel in his fist, a load of mortar on his shoulder, or the sanitary inspector making marginal notes on a Wagner score. This was surely one form of originality, but it daunted the least adventurous and actually drove some to suicide, all their golden hopes dashed, their promises betrayed. I persisted, having nothing else to hope for, but my Treischnitt and

61

Kolberhoff forays never paid off like the old ones, and I had to make up my mind without the least guidance or advice. After a while, I began to hear non-conversations from them, Treischnitt telling Kolberhoff to say something to me, and then telling him to tell me he had said nothing at all, closely followed by Kolberhoff telling Treischnitt to tell me something he'd said and soon after telling him to tell me he'd said nothing at all. Then I heard them in unison, telling each other to tell me something they had said or wanted to say, and then cancelling it by telling each other to tell me that they had not said it at all. This was the Great Oral Wall of China. Past this there was no going, was there? I suppose that, if their disappearance had been more than a merely token one, I might have gone around Vienna asking if anyone had seen a tall man and a shortish one both agitatedly discussing, as any pair of Switzerland-lovers might, the Piano Concertino of Arthur Honegger, in which Kolberhoff had discerned the constant attempts of tiny horses to mount from the framework of the pianoforte to the actual keys, but forever sliding back, these horses miniature in the most drastic way: the size of a thumbnail, with the nimblest, plodding little feet you ever saw, but condemned to jump up to the keyboard and there prance for the rest of their lives. This constant movement of theirs the music enacted, he claimed, in rhythms both easy-going and strenuous, the whole done with tender delicacy. How typical of Kolber-hoff to indulge such a pipedream, to apprehend what, properly speaking, was nowhere in the music proper, any more than Switzerland was in Vienna. This cosmopoli-tanism of his irked many people, Treischnitt included, of course, but he kept it going all the same, stoking up his absentee heart with this or that cultural reference until, well if you saw him enough, you could stand no more. Above all, almost as an echo of his visionary mishearings or misplacings, he was a lover of anachronism (word I al-ways split up into ana- and -chronism to make life easier), implanting the future in the past to a weird extent merely to indicate the fear and trembling with which he like so many Viennese confronted what I called the End-Zeit, the End of Time, or the End of our Time. Thus he would bring what was going to happen into the conversation of teatime, not that I was invited to any such thing. But you heard, to be sure, of his peculiar habits, eventually having to reconcile yourself to them in the abstract, to the legend of his fearsome eccentricity in private—his fear of fruit, say, or his unholy fascination with mashed potato, a sachet of this powder always within reach lest an emergency overtake him. To myself, I called these odd habits of his absentee exflux, akin to what I had heard elsewhere at a table in some dingy hostel: the domestic form of emigration, yet another way of ducking the End-Zeit that polluted the Viennese air, marred relationships, and drove all kinds of people to bewitched modulations of homely behavior. His Honegger, his tiny horses, were an escape hatch he would have liked to share, but, as the saying went, there was only room for one in there, no matter how much he talked about the composer and the Concertino in fantastic deployments of misplaced taste. I ask you while, presumably, you are still there and have not slunk away to purchase fried basset hound with pasta or whatever else you use to keep body and soul together, unlike Treischnitt and Kolberhoff who seemed to have given up altogether the habit of eating: not a pickle, not a schnitzel, never a beet, nor even a torte. What was I to make of abstemious absentees paid a fortune to flout the very job they were appointed to by, presumably, royal charter and the everloving Academy where the experts joined free hands at urinal troughs, heedless of their esthetic preferences. I cruised the streets chanting, Come home, Treischnitt, come home, Kolberhoff, all is forgiven, my dears, but I was forever being urged to move on, and whenever I sang from within my niche opposite the Terza Rima they winkled me out even from that, as if I had a shank secreted on me to plunge into any given diner at

random. Now the Academy ran itself, I presumed, its sec-
retaries still there but quite cut off from the folk they
ministered to, pleasing themselves about money and public lectures. No flag flew at half staff, no funereal music
poured through the hallways, not even the toilets were
closed in their honor. I gave up and concentrated on my
new work, the casual glimpse of ancient Vienna with
which to awe them.

This was a view of a bulwark

THIS WAS A VIEW OF A BULWARK or a balustrade, some steps and an archway, roofs and chimneys: modest picture postcard stuff such as they clearly, in their palsy-walsy way, preferred, the fundamental architecture as exposed as a pelvis yet screened to the right by advertisements plastered all over a wall. I don't mean that, otherwise the wall in all its nakedness would have screened the rest of it. I mean the advertisements seemed to exceed themselves, get out of hand, leaking over to the left, so much so that you half-expected them to grow like lettuces and take over the entire scene, which they no doubt one day would. I wondered if Treischnitt might exclaim to Kolberhoff this was just the kind of thing they wanted, or Kolberhoff to Treischnitt, in whichever of their shady hideaways they happened to be. Nothing baronial here, just a lot of masonry defaced, as required by the decline and fall of the West. An inoffensive view, this, it had only one soul in sight and she far distant up two flights of steps in the middle distance, swollen from the waist down, stranded in a huge apron: Frau Treischnitt, Frau Kolberhoff, I would hazard a guess. A lady who, installed in her house, the thing built around her, could not get out again. The rest of the area is pure of people. Is that what they want? My problem, singular, is that I do not listen to them for very long, whereas those whom I encounter in my lodgings listen to me for hours on end, eager for rant and rave, having nothing better to do. I never seem to run out of complaints, which makes me sound like a hypochondriac, but I merely mean grievances, in which as I grow older I abound, just from wondering what I will have to do next in order to survive on bowls of soup, hunks of bread: the true artist's life. Perhaps my future will be posters, hair tonic, bed-feathers, some murderous antiperspirant called Teddy, in which my own special brand of people, mailmen or draymen, wring out their socks to mop their brows with, then powder their feet before resuming. Then there is always soap, they always need soap, much as they need cafés, little outdoor abattoirs at which to read free newspapers, I mean newspapers for free. I too. All the time, whether frustrated or overlooked, I thought of my life as a tributary flowing into the mighty Danube of power, prowess, and world fame, unstoppable even when slinking drop by drop from higher up to lower down, where the resplendent world was. Another little Wagner coming to pre-eminence from behind a heap of soapy posters. If you think this way for long, you begin to twitch, you tell all to a gang of cronies who don't matter, and fail to get on with your work, meaning what your soul demands, not what keeps you alive from day to day: a crust, a porridge a gruel, a scraped-out jar of marmalade. So there I am, with ten chimneys, eleven windows, twelve steps (had I calculated it all so well?), countless tiles, and two picket fences, a typical old Vienna scene, yet just as typical I supposed as of Munich, Sofia, London. Who knew? How I labored at it, getting it right, smudging and shading, softening with a thumb-rub or a touch of the eraser, so easy to wipe out, to replace, left in pencil or charcoal so as to suit the examiners' pleasure. It was a watercolor, really, but minus its colors so far, *detained,* as the British loved to say about the condemned, *during Her Majesty's Pleasure,* at least in the Victorian period, when they kept on falling through the drop with that big knot to one side of their neck. Little did the English know of the so-called Austrian method: strangulation with a thin hempen cord, easily a twenty-minute procedure I was reserving for Treischnitt and Kolberhoff, but only after we had poached their balls and

eyeballs in those cute little purple cups you fill with bo-
racic to bathe your eyes in. A poacher I would be. If anything the work in question was too full—none of that
open wasteland. in front of a palace, but buildings bumping into buildings, everything hemmed in as if designed
by someone endowed with fanatical powers of concen-
tration. Could this be 1911? It was. Not that the date mattered, what mattered was how Treischnitt, that old faker,
and Kolberhoff, that other old faker, would respond, if
they even took the trouble to peer at it much, arbiters of
the Fisher King Fellowships, about which I the inveterate
devourer of newspapers had never seen a word in print. It
was always like that: you heard about something supposedly famous, and then all mention of it ceased, leading
you to believe that anything you heard of was not real but
merely conjured into rumor by those intent on doing you
harm. What could I do, trapped between unavailable trophies and proffered rubbish? I could just hear Treischnitt
telling Kolberhoff to tell him to deny me, and Kolberhoff
doing so, only for Treischnitt, my minimal savior, to tell
him he had said no such thing and the blame was all Kolberhoff's. Take that, I told myself. The stuffing speaks for
the doll. Into the sky the chimneys puffed a pinkish, no a
blueish concoction, bloody or inky, you follow the trac-
tion of my hand in this? Do they want smoke? Is there

smoke in their world? Cremated, would they go up in
smoke or merely evaporate like two addled fairies? It was
not for me to know, not the likes of me, not so much
working-class (see my father's glorious aspirations) as
lower middle, with cultural dreams to my credit, high-
flown Wagnerian idylls soaring through my skull. In the
world I adored, that England south of the Trent, were
there not, at those ancient seats of learning, Oxford and
Cambridge, never said as Cambridge and Oxford (Kolberschnitt would know why), special scholarships of the
most restricted sort, offered to sons of clergymen born
south of the Thames whose fathers had spent at least a
year in Pernambuco? Very closed, these awards, but it was
possible for the only qualified person in the whole country to catch up with his award, so to speak, and thus
launch on a distinguished career only he could have.
Imagine the day the youth heard he was unique and his
uniqueness had already been catered for. If there was an
award for a boy who looked like an ox, then he would
have it. Or like a cam. How wonderful to have in mind a
country ideal as a dewdrop, so much so that you want
them to invade your own and take you over, snuggling
you into the empire among all that pink on the map. Life
had not worked out that way, but I prayed that, whatever
became of Vienna, my adopted home (as a flea inhabits a

73

dog), we would never come into conflict with the land of
the Widow of Windsor as I called her. She was no longer
there in 1911, of course, but her impress was: where she
had sat, eaten, done her number twos. How could one
abandon Vienna? Only in order to go to London, say. It
was as simple and as impossible as that. Did the realm of
the Fisher King extend that far? Were there, say, traveling
fellowships for young Viennese, tenable at Ox or Cam, so
as to make gentlemen out of languid foreigners? How I
aspired to be a gentleman in bowler hat, with pin-striped
pants and natty umbrella, a pearl in my silver silk tie, my
habitual speech a highly modulated bray, all my sentences
beginning with that classic English overture: *I say....* They
ask in negatives, I am told: *I don't suppose you have a ticket
to Capetown. Oh you do, then I don't suppose you would go so
far as to sell it to me?* You are bound to get on when you are
that suave. Does it take a lifetime to become that well-
bred? Or may there, o Treischnitt, o Kolberhoff, be a
weekend course in the subject, conducted in German,
just to get us started? Free only to Fisher King Fellows,
visionaries of the streets, loiterers from the Terza Rima,
winnowers of the smartest conversation in the land. You
can see the depth of my yearning, how much I was willing to sacrifice merely to get away and stroll along the
Thames with an independent air. My day would come, I

knew, and there I would be, Fellow of the British Academy, habitué of the Coldstream Guards, frequenter of Buckingham Palace, member of the Order of Merit, flaunter of the Order of the Garter. I could see an imperial future beckoning me, provided I handled the Treischnitts and Kolberhoffs well, kept away from their stoops in the suburbs, and somehow pitched the entire exchange at a high level of fastidious discourse interrupted by not a single work of my art. It all had to be made abstract, I thought, so as to give no offence (I longed to spell in the *English* way) or if giving offense, at least at once referring the matter to seconds and a box of pistols. That sort of honorable, chaste life, sweetly agreeable, as they used to say. I was against the crude, the crass, the exaggerated. I was not a Norwegian. I was not roses. I was sooner or later to be paralyzed by the vision of my own greatness while Vienna fell apart, sundered by too many nations in its breadbasket, and allowed no future but that of a heifer with decorated flanks. Communications in the old days, it is said, were more than difficult, and in the early twentieth century they were not so good. When I wished to say something to Treischnitt, I often spoke to him directly, or to Kolberhoff if I wished to say something to *him;* but sometimes I would say to Kolberhoff what I wished to say to Treischnitt, and to Treischnitt what I wanted to say to

Kolberhoff. This was orderly. Sometimes, however, I would want to say something to Treischnitt when Treischnitt was not there, so I said it to Kolberhoff, hoping, and sometimes I had to say, hoping, to Treischnitt what I wanted to say to the missing Kolberhoff. At other times what I wished to say I wished to say to them both, to both Treischnitt and Kolberhoff, when I spoke more loudly if both were present, but when only one was present, say Treischnitt not Kolberhoff, or Kolberhoff not Treischnitt, I was reduced to the oblique stance of talking to them indirectly, although there was a world of difference between addressing myself to one of two, both present, and one of two, one being absent, thus reducing the chances of innuendo, mannerism, or facial tic. Even worse, sometimes they were both absent when I wanted to speak to either or to both, and the wise course would have been to leave a message in pencil, or in blood on a shoebox, but what I did instead, quite often, was address myself to vacancy, which was better than saying nothing at all to either the space customarily occupied by Treischnitt or by Kolberhoff, and I used to wonder what was keeping them from me and what I had to say. Never could I see myself as talking to *myself*. No fear. Perhaps I am a muddlehead; the question would only arise, so to speak, when I was invading a small country and some wide-awake person had said

turn right at France, or left at Hungary, or when I was
conversing, you guessed it, with Treischnitt and Kolberhoff, and I remained unsure if Treischnitt or Kolberhoff
had said a certain thing, I remaining unsure of whom to
ask, Treischnitt or Kolberhoff, about it. This is to say that,
even when others were present at these two-way or
three-way exchanges, the level of Treischnitt-reporting or
Kolberhoff-reporting was not very high. There was a lot
of *I thought he had said it but he denies it,* and of *I'm never
very sure when I'm tired,* Treischnitt or Kolberhoff letting it
out with a huge sigh. It was almost as if those squeezers
and benders at the post office had decided to maul the
spoken instead of the written word. So they mauled Treischnitt and Kolberhoff, who had the trick of throwing
their voices, or Treischnitt of sounding like Kolberhoff
and Kolberhoff of sounding like Treischnitt, though nary
a duet broke free from them, it would have been too
bourgeois an act, more appropriate to a barbershop quar-
tet. I had long ago concluded the aim of all they said was
to bamboozle everybody, to keep things secret, even
when they pretended to be helpful, with all kinds of ami-
able little interjections (*If I may; let me help; this is how*), not
to mention *A-ha* and *Oh boy,* which raise the heart no
end. Keeping things clear and in the simple language of
the longtime civil servant, say, was always a problem, as

was the business of making sure you said to Treischnitt
your Treischnittiana and to Kolberhoff your Kolberhoffiana. I may have come from the provinces, or indeed the
country, but I was not a bumpkin or a lummock. Words
from me slid down and away like loaves on a sinking ship,
and I could tell that people waited for me to announce
myself as Muggins: *Muggins is here,* meaning the half-wit
had arrived and was free for making fun of. I had not, I
suppose, had much human experience, only later realizing
how easy it was to have someone executed; all that was
needed was a scrap of paper signed. As it was, whenever I
encountered one of those cellophane sheaths that Vienna
bread sometimes came in (a French influence), and I slid
my hand and wrist and arm in deep to grab an end to tear
off in my curmudgeon-like way, I was reminded of the
farm, when the cowherd or the animal doctor clad his
arm in a long rubber gauntlet before plunging it all the
way into the bouncing innards of a cow. Such a life that
was. Nobody in Vienna would believe such things, although I did notice now and then how that little appetizer, two shrimps head to tail on a dais of chopped fennel, got itself known as "a sex," since the arrangement, as
I learned, corresponded to 69, which added up to 15,
which added up to six, or *sex* in German. The intricate
mysteries of Viennese cuisine left me standing; I felt like

a window cleaner at the Pyramids, wondering how to escape. The thought that ceaselessly haunts my untidy brain is this: never mind how much you take care of your health, something terrible is going to happen to you sooner or later. You are going to be ravaged, broken up, made to rot, and you might as well get used to the concept, staving off the evil day as long as possible. Yet there is something to be said, especially among the clean-shaven, for how whiskers yield to the razor better after a meal, I know not why, so shouldn't we take advantage of that fact as a minor consolation? I don't mean rush away and shave right now, or rush away to eat in order to shave, but consider it next time, so that you become like so many of us at ease in your dreadfulness. This is the way God wanted it, take it or leave it; the success of the universe appears to depend on billions of broken hearts. Now this is worse than my companion Henisch asking what my occupation was and, on being told "painter," saying oh that's good, you'll find plenty of work at such a trade. I was insulted, not a house painter, but an artist, and not an academician either, one in league with the free spontaneity of the imagination. Imagine, then, my beginning to copy (Henisch's idea) old postcards and lithographs of Viennese beauty spots, which he then sold to dealers, framers, upholsterers, who carefully attached

them to the backs of couches or easy chairs. Such a fate
for an artist whose scruffy clothes exempted him from
going out socially prompts me to wonder what I can do
for Henisch, in another life, when there are no more prof-
its to share 50-50. That image of my copywork being slid
into the high backs of what people sat on disturbs me.
Were they ever aware of what lay and flourished behind
them in seductive tints, making of them semi-sandwich
people (old way of advertising not confined to Vienna)?
Did it warm them to know that a gifted young artist, one
devoted to *Kunst,* had slaved away at a copy that would be
tacked on to a chair back just to relieve the boredom of
looking at plain wood? Would my copies not have fared
better at the front, so that the Viennese rested their backs
on the real thing, no doubt creasing it and wearing it
away, yet in contact with something real for the human
touch grafted onto it? Oh, recoiling from the surface, they
would cry, what have I squashed behind me? An insect?
No, it is one of those charming piccies they install to
guarantee that nobody looks at them, there is always a human being in the way, taking his or her ease with a fairly
straight back. Better, surely, to glue Vienna scenes over
their genitals, a sort of figleaf figment, to advertise the
place where their brains live. Again, I have hopes for the
wheedling, devious Henisch, intent not so much on

80

gleaning me some cash as on finding an easy humiliation for me right there in the flophouse we shared. I promised myself to catch up with him in the afterlife, setting him to work on the backs of upright chairs, so as to remind him of the good old days when we weren't too proud to beg. Having become a diligent skimmer of newspapers, in hostel or café, more probably *at* café, I had begun to notice how the game was played, picking up here a line or two from Treischnitt, who claimed that a certain Poleisterman misused diagonals, as Kleister had already suggested, though Kleister had also followed Prinzlamp's suggestion that Poleisterman really needed glasses. It went on like that, sometimes sinking lower than usual, as when Kolberhoff in an interview derided Poleisterman as a pseudo-Jew, whatever that meant, whose real name was Dohnanyi. It must have felt good to them to get among their fellow speedboats like this, doing one another in, hammering Lithuanians and Finns, lauding Germans and Swedes, or whoever was out, in, that particular day. Torpedoing. Sinking. Slicing in two with the propeller. I had missed all these zoo antics of the art profession, though I knew of the various sects, none of whom spoke to the others, having disagreed about pastels, canvas, and chalk. It never took much to get them started, and there had so far been nothing big enough to stop them. Few of these squabblers did any creative work, which would have wasted bickering-time, of course, so they had to argue about work from the past, skulls exhumed from the boneyard of their own failures while energetic young fellows such as I, full of initiative, stayed on the sidelines ignored, dumb enough to draw and paint when quarrels were the vogue. Small wonder I sold out. Denizens of Outre-Tombe, from beyond the grave, are always tempted to report as if from immediately after what happened, with no knowledge of Outre-Tombe at all, as if they never knew they had a complete life and a death. The temptation is there, to hand all over to the first twenty years, or thirty, and have done, the whole thing couched in a language of foreshortened innocence. My own way, however, as a denizen of OT (DOT) is to make myself free to use all idioms of any era, to become the freemason of my own memory, and the heir of all the ages, their idioms and slang, thus widening my perspective. OT may not have many perks (see), but one of them is surely the right to know everything, especially things post-mortem, as in the best literature. It is the imagination that reigns, not the mortician, though he too learns more about you, after you have "gone," than you knew yourself. So, ghosts are not limited to their era's idioms, or even to those of their own lives, but range far and wide, opining and divining, tenderer to their tenseless fits than you would ever have expected, harsher to their failures, gentler to their enemies, harsher to their friends. What a circus the inquest becomes as we try to be precise, bumping noses with other occupants of course, some of whom we recognize (Wagner, Pfitzner, Bartók). It is all a matter of self-discipline: offered the long-awaited all, we have to be eclectic, not making a meal of it, yet getting across how it felt to be me just then, and not bothering with the years of glory: in other words, an understated study. I must have been well-behaved in those Vienna days: not a single black eye, not a single split lip. Not that there was never provocation, always someone saying you are so prolific, whatever that meant, or you seem to be in everyone's good books, or you seem to manage to agree with everybody, and you keep working while the rest of us are trying to develop a philosophy of life—this meaning I was empty-headed. I struck nobody, though I made a mental list of those who stimulated me with their quips and sarcasms. There are always those around you who, on principle, despise you on the grounds of where you came from, Murmansk or the Moon, as well as those who take it as a mortal insult whenever you touch paint to paper. These nay-sayers besiege every life, garbing their hatred in faint praise, lauding your deportment or your courtesy while envying your productivity, even if it be merely copies of ancient postcards. The broken glass of acquaintanceship, dreadful word for a gruesome concept, remains in your skin unless you make it a weekend habit to tease it out. Henisch especially was always trying to put me up to something in the belief that whatever I was already doing wasn't worthwhile. Agitator-pawnbroker, he. I moved on, celebrant of my own bright lights. There in the city of jollity and the waltz I kept an eye open for Slavs and Jews, social democrats and the House of Hapsburg, not to mention the heirs of Treischnitt and Kolberhoff. With the two of them I was already enmeshed, too far to withdraw. If you lived in Vienna, without being Viennese — well, that sums it up. To be Viennese was to affect a mindless light-heartedness, an insouciance of privileged vacuity, but I was never able to rise to such balderdash and folly, letting my serious streak take over. For a while I tinkered with model planes, putting them together with butter-fingered zeal, then stationing them against the lamplight at various angles to pretend an attack or a reconnaissance was under way. I had even toyed with the idea of trying to design full-sized aircraft and becoming the owner of an enormous factory that yielded a gross profit. Truth told, I was only one of thousands envisioned in Frank Wedekind's *The Awakening of Spring* and Robert Musil's *Young Törless,*

in which idealistic young men turned against the bourgeois habits of their fathers and plumped for the arts.
How spiritual we all were, an entire generation of the dis-
abused, equally tempted by suicide and greatness. Yet I
suppose, for my fervor, and the degree of it, I was unique,
no run-of-the-mill rebel but one almost crippled by his
own superfine emotions, too sensitive to the world to endure it, yet somehow clinging on by his fingernails for the
great days to begin, in which I would rid myself of the
Treischnitts and Kolberhoffs who ran everything into the
ground, Viennese style of course, with airy hypocrisy.
When you grow up feeling you are too good for the
world, and, once you are "up," continue to feel so, you run
into the worst opposition of all, with people calling you a
vegetable imbecile, a blathering parasite, a performing
flea, out of sheer envy that you never sold out. It then becomes murderously hard to stick to your beliefs and sol-
dier on, a point at which so many abolish themselves into
the military, say, or the external shell of a bourgeois job
merely to provide bread and light. To continue taking the
world on the chin, you need to be some kind of boxer,
open to attack because always attacking, vulnerable to the
counterpunch because always punching—jabbing and
feinting. When the divine Wagner gets called a charlatan
barber, an addict of banality, the headwaiter of music, then

you know the gloves are off and the knuckledusters on. A bloody nose becomes your coat of arms, easily recognized by your fellows, and you endure the rebuffs of the Treischnitts and the Kolberhoffs—those purveyors of the inherited divine right to control everything—in the sanguine belief that they will die away, buried with their shameless autobiographies and their list of insults: Don't you understand, sir, that to be an artist you must begin with a modicum of taste, a ship's hold full of flair? Stuff like that has held the world back for centuries, when sheer hatred of the Other has driven gifted men to suicide and madness. Officious meddling will never die out, but in those days the past masters of it were getting away with murder, the Treischnitts and Kolberhoffs licking their own fart-juice in palatial apartments disguised as helpful offices, the only other audible sound the tee-hee of proud power. To have grown to manhood surrounded by such oafs was a feat of some kind, but I always aimed forward, even when in pain, *managing* with postcards but ever attentive to the glorious surges within me that kept saying to my hand, my wrist, This is how to do it, this is the exact style the world in its serious, spiritual way has been waiting for. The great thing about such an intense intellectual maturation as mine was that, even if it came to naught and I somehow did not become the recognized artistic genius I aspired to be, I would still have had that priceless advantage of, well, an intense intellectual maturation. It stands to reason that everyone eligible should be groomed to this magical point, either to go on to genius or, held back, to buttress the foundations of the genius-sustaining élite. Trying to paint a view of the Vienna Parliament building, I told Henisch it would be an Hellenic masterpiece on Austrian soil, so I told him to get me fifty crowns for it, but he came up with only ten, having pocketed the other forty. So I took him to court and got him seven days for his labor. The odd thing was that the buyer's widow was all ready to testify that only ten crowns had changed hands. I often wondered why Henisch, passing himself off as Fritz Walter, never called her as a witness. This was how I fell into the clutches of a certain Franz Neumann living in the same hostel as Henisch-Walter and myself. This Jew, Neumann, or I myself, or he and I went hawking my work all over Vienna, just like big-game hunters on safari (a word invented for the masses by an English exotophile named Burton). In truth, of course, we were pimp and prostitute, eager for crowns, indifferent to how we were treated. You can only take so much before you caseharden and tell yourself just one more year of this and I will be free, treading with a lilt on the bright veldt of fame. I took note of the squalor around me, but never turned it into a philosophical emblem, content to dream my way into the future, head full of music, my eyes surfeited with the beauty of my own creations, while the profiteering minions, Treischnitt and Kolberhoff, even Henisch and Neumann, fell away into the gutter where they belonged, mere agents of a foreign power called greed. Was it then or later that the correct rhetoric for all this human wastage formed and settled in my head, at the tip of my tongue, a vocabulary mostly evocative of pigs and rats; square snouts, the swinish pack of parsons, all the dung-art of the East and the Americas. Such are the maneuvers of the man of taste crucified. He howls that the world may notice him and, later, come to relish the work he accomplished during his years of torment, judging his cries of desperation as the leitmotifs they truly were, the ripe emblems in the symphony of his too-tender life. To have had a life of any sort was a triumph, but to have managed to keep it aesthetic amid the snarling panthers and the beaming frauds was an act of genius. It was to *Kunst,* holy heavenly *Kunst* I gave myself. That is one way of summing up a life, akin to (presumably) Kolberhoff's crack about Treischnitt: He didn't wait for me, and that was after losing interest in his skies, in which I had always taken an interest for *his* sake. Friendship among men, Kolberhoff was always saying, is as fungus in

a whirlwind—where there is no loyalty. So Kolberhoff. I
often wondered if these cracks of his, ostensibly against
Treischnitt, even during his final illness, were really aimed
at me, who gushed loyalty all over the place and devoured
friendship like a mongrel of the streets, even risking a bite
or six for the sake of it. In the end, I had to file this and
other worries under what I called my theory of knowledge, the core of which was that humans do not need
very accurate knowledge at all. Rumor will always do, as
with such vexed topics as the Polish attitude to Jews, especially in farming districts, the role of Jews in German
and Austrian publishing houses, the neededness of a military aristocracy in any national army, the effect of poor
sight on the history of European painting, the impact of
syphilis on Platonic thinkers, the role of impotence in
child molesters. And so forth. It is a waste of time looking
such matters up in order to get the final word. People do
not need the final word, but a final-*seeming* word couched
in bold, convincing language that wants to be believed.
People want to think they know, and whether or not they
do know is beside the point if that feeling of knowing
gets them into action. So be it in the best of possible
worlds. Like all good things, it is in the mind it really
counts. Yet, no matter how much you feel you have given
yourself unstintingly, you never lose the fact of already

having been given, and no matter what you accomplish you are destined to be shredded up like oranges for marmalade. No: worse—for nothing really, just in the interests of destruction. I wouldn't put it past the universe to have secreted, say, a Treischnitt somewhere in Ethiopia in a glue factory, just for the sake of saving him, where no doubt he is not glad but resentful at having been saved not as a king, a prince, some loathsome potentate. I would never put it past the universe to save some rotter on the quiet, just for show, to encourage all the others, the Wagners and even Frederick the Great, all of us hoping to be the one exempted, but no qualification enough to face down the obtuse need to ruin us just as we are getting into our stride. The universe is that kind of place, gentlemen, don't underestimate its prejudice against us, proving we have always been a fluke, a by-blow. So the chance of rising in your career with a prospect of finally running things for the next thousand years recedes into the routine of dust, and all that is left is names, dates, doings, the chaff of endless and pointless commentary. So why bother with a career, I ask you, all that labor and humiliation, when it is bound to be nipped in the bud or cut off in full bloom? The universe fobs us off with the means of killing time rather than the serious materials of a worthwhile destiny. You can't have everything, but you might well want more than most men. The question then arises, even when put to such spent forces as Treischnitt and Kolberhoff, of why we should not behave like the universe itself, cutting and mowing, not behaving well to our fellow creatures but annihilating them to give the good old universe a helping hand, in its dirty work? They who destroy the most lives, not the Treischnitts and the Kolberhoffs, mere amateurs at this, but the Attilas, they are the ones who perhaps come closest to winning cosmic favor, considered for eternity but rejected at the last as not quite universal enough, although, well, B+ for effort. You can see how a sensitive, brooding individual who feels he has been shortchanged in the Vienna swap-shop, begins to torture himself with the dead old question of why bother? Merely to carve a scar on the universe. Unless, the few exempted from the pointless ritual of death secrete themselves with huge resolve where they will never be found. Were they to be exposed as having been let off, surely they would be torn to shreds on the spot out of sheer resentment. They would hardly have a chance to found a new religion, say, or the best political party ever known. I do begin to believe, however, that a few may be living among us, cached away to no purpose, but spared by the universe just for the sake of doing it. I have my hopes therefore. Even if this present act be all there is to it, orating to the mind's ear in a shower of panic. It is not Outre Tombe after all but the promised land unrecognized as such because your expectations are too great, not humble enough. Why, this is immortality, to take it out in talk. The snag of course, is what I call the dastardly penumbra, sibling of the umbra and all that lurks in it. There is what happened. Then, next to it in the half-shadow, the stuff that followed, and next to that in the penumbra—the almost shadow—everything else. Perhaps I have it wrong and the umbra is darkest of the three. It matters little, I am recalling my art days as clearest in mind, all the way up to the war that ensued, and then after that—what? A mess of endeavor I see unclearly and have no wish to resurrect. No, this is the epic of Treischnitt and Kolberhoff, who both made and unmade it, my Fisher King fellowship never having materialized, my second examination, if such, never taking place, neither man taking the time to view that lovely Old Vienna scene of mine with all the chimneys and posters. I was left floating free, able to make up my own mind about postcards, or briefly taking a construction job that brought back to life my passion for architecture. In those days I lived in imagined palaces, I basked in dreams, ever ready to be beaten up by fellow men unable to understand the zeal I brought to all I touched. If there is no beyond to what you do, your life has settled down into the size and scope of a postage stamp, and you have to hasten to unpeel yourself from whatever you have become attached to, not so much the Treischnitts and the Kolberhoffs, lords and masters of your fate, but the whole murderous, vapid city that is dragging you down, not because you have poor taste or a rotten gift, because neither applies, but out of sheer tradition and experiment. They want you to fail because the city always depends on there being a majority of failures, never mind who they are, so long as there are plenty of them. They do this to you not because you lurk opposite the Terza Rima, or copy old postcards, or take no sass from the Henisches, but because the machinery for your degradation has always been there, like an old guillotine in the corner of the execution shed, not to be *un-*invented but brought into play merely to be useful. Trei- and Kolb– happen merely to be instruments of some bigger force, disguised as patrons of beauty, or whatever else, but there to serve lest they themselves get chopped. off. I did not arrive in order to ruin Vienna, or even to wish it ill, but merely to become another uninvited scuttling ant.

The Dry Danube

Why doesn't he go to Iceland or Peru? You know how that sounds, that sort of aimless abusive question. Not designed to hearten you, any more than the weather, it has a more than suffocating effect, interesting you in power for the first time in your life, even though you arrived as a nascent aesthete, an idolizer of the great creators of the past. You are bound sooner or later to undergo the conversion, having fed yourself into the engine. Nothing was more muddled or lethal than the Vienna of those days, source of the nihilistic Schadenfreude that occurs even now in the popular ditties of the neighborhood—if I dare:

> There was a young man of Vienna
>> Who cleaned out his body with senna.
>> He turned out so thin
>> They sheathed him with tin
> And use him now as an antenna.

I am not even clear what it means, or after whom it can be modeled, but it haunts the streets, to no purpose, and will die out as everything else dies too. I think I have the words rather garbled, but they no doubt began garbled, and they do come from the penumbra, that shady zone in which neither history nor memoir is precise, where everything, as I understand it, is almost but not quite in the deepest shadow of all. There is what is real, Vienna of then, then the shadow stuff, next to the rest which, not quite in the darkest zone, remains vague and uncited. That is how Outre Tombe strands you in your own memory, and you have no more heart to continue than if you were shipwrecked on Jupiter. I had always thought that, at some suitable point, I would discover the paragraph, its uses and joys, making what you say available like the courses in a meal, but no, it has never come my way and it doubtless will not. As ever I am trapped in a splurge, with nothing in the right order, almost no combination of cause with effect, but with an overriding sense of having been wounded, a walking mutilé de some guerre, as the French so conveniently put it in their Métro system. I was a mutilé de la paix, so to speak, driven out like dock-yard scum when all I wanted to be was a Treischnitt or a Kolberhoff, even to the extent of having Frau T. or Frau K. to contend with up in the Alps with a huge can of lard to cook them in. Those would have been the days. I would have been better off in that erection-provoking mountain air with some bronzed, deep-chested Bavarian girl given to hiking and climbing in lederhosen, but it never happened, though I do recall certain eventful passages in my early days. I just wanted to become a credit to my upbringing instead of having my work scattered

95

about Vienna, in this or that poky little shop, as the true diaspora of a genius. Summoning it all together is an impossible task, unless you happen to be the Van Gogh who rhymes with *mango,* mispronounced by the winners when it should be pronounced as spelled. Ah, the public, heaven help it in its culture throes. The round slot in my head that functions as a letterbox, American style, sometimes receives (it has no options) doggerel of the most appalling variety, either aimed at me or designed to implicate me, as if I still cared. I suppose this amounts to having met my public at long last:

> There was a young eunuch of Munich
>> Who spilled some hot sperm on his tunic.
>> He washed it with Lysol
>> But got a bad eyeful,
> So now he's the *blind* eunuch of Munich.

Popular art is no respecter of persons, though why such as I should volunteer to be the butt of such scurrility I do not know. This is the smutty world of the postcard getting its own back, and distinctly American in tone. Back to Duluth with all of them. Retaliate? Never. In through one ear and out through the other, *meine Herren.* Once a Viennese, always, I suppose. To fight back has always been

a compliment. I do not recall having written an autobiography, and I do not propose to embark on it now, but
rather to let the sewer of history drain its gruesome way
through me, as if I were a grating in the Ringstrasse. If I
come at all it is in history's face. Strolling would be beside
the point, like orating, peering in windows, slinking to
the nonexistent Terza Rima, peering at postcards of ero-
tomania. I want none of this, only to be left alone, an
unseduced revenant. You never know that, if you come
back at all, or if a little snippet of you comes back, it goes
to the place where you were least happy. Now, that's a ma-
licious universe for you. So you decline into being an
anxious, anchored voice, asking your Horatio to report
you aright to the world (and any other ratio that happens
along). What did Frau Röntgen say when she saw her
ring in the first X-ray picture, bold on her skeletal hand?
I have seen my death, she said, Frau Röntgen said, but she
had also seen her life. The skeleton of a living hand is no
more morbid than a dead diamond. But you can see what
Frau Röntgen was driving at: the shock, the revelation,
the weird image the rays brought into being. She meant,
not *I have seen my death* but the secret nature of life itself,
lurking there, laughing at us all, telling us it's our friend
for a while but will survive us, as bones always do. We do

not want to be ridiculed after we have gone, not that it
matters much; we just do not fancy post-mortem guf-
faws, making light of our heaviest aspirations as we settle
down in our graves and urns like the fellows of the
Oxford and Cambridge colleges wrapping their gowns
around them while dining in Hall on a particularly drafty
night or appraising the port and lager, chops and venison
during a mellow summer. Those are the scenes that tell us
what sort of a life we might have had, peacefully brooding on the classics, our main worry rust on a beloved bicycle parked in the porter's lodge. I go to these exotic al-
bum entries for fear that something else break through,
rupturing the brittle illusion that we have been happy and
lived the right life, defying even our best friends, our parents, our siblings, the totality of those who, dead or alive,
will always be heard, muttering, carping, complaining,
chiding, getting to you as best they can: Why, you're a—
I've half a mind to dust your pants. That's what I said.
Some mothers do have them. Have what? Well, if you
don't know, there's no point in telling you. As I said,
you're a—as I said before. Now don't you come it.
Enough is more than too much. I'll—You'll what? Well,
I won't then, but you'd better watch out. Don't you come
it. I'll please myself, that's what I'll do, I've always done
that. How does it go? What's its name when it's at home?
I'll box your ears, that I will. Just let me—What? Never

you mind, I'll larrup you. I'm safe as houses, you would-
n't dare. Wouldn't I? There's them that do and them that
don't. Don't you come it, you fast mover. Once I get set,
I'll be having you and giving you what for. You and who
else? Me with myself, that's all it takes, loudmouth. You
and whose mother? Don 't you come it. It'll rain or go
dark before morning. Well, you don't know everything. I
don't need to with such as you around, ever more stupid
one day after another. I'll be keeping an eye on you. And
I on you. We'll see who gets larruping. You'd better watch
your mouth. Put wood in that hole. There's no knowing.
I'm not going to stand for it. There's thousands wouldn't.
And the English actually have a place called Grimethorpe
and another called Scumthorpe. It's Scunthorpe. Just as
bad. That's where. You see if you don't. I'll be having you.
Safe as houses. Stick it up your jumper, then, and see then.
The more you eat, the more you trump. My whole life
was like that, an endless fanfare. If I come over there,
you'll wish I hadn't. You and whose army? Never you
mind, shiteface. You'll mind, I'll give you a piece of my
mind proper, that I will, messmouth. Don't you come it.
I've already come it. Stands to reason. Don't you reason
me. You'll get it in the chops you will. Me and who else?
Just you, you little rubbish heap. Well, be told. I've told
you. I won't tell you again. Don't. Don't you try it, ma-
nure cake. I'll please myself, come what may. Don't you

dare. I'm a daredevil I am. You'll soon be nothing at all. Amid the extreme nature of the things they did, these exchanges had a poisonous, demented quality they might all have regretted if only they had time to reflect on the vulnerability of humanity and, come to think of it, the bird population too, the elks, the skunks, the lions, the polar bears, the very centipedes. Calm down then and we'll have a better going on. They never did. I was always being abused by people in order to make me abuse them. It happens when astride the cycle of history, you perch your backside on the seat and it wears you sore over the first few miles, making you wriggle until you realize there will never be a comfortable position to ride in. The bicycle has its way downhill with you and you cling on for life, teetering, the seat tears away, and you are seated on the erect metal tube under it, unable to sit down at all. It is the end of the ride. Such the result of being within a civilization at all. Better to have inhabited a cloud and be obliged to its cantankerous household gods, making your way freely according to your own lights. What a paradox that the aesthetic impulse manages to get itself born, but almost as soon as watered and beginning to bud made to behave, told how to perform—why? Because there are always people who like to tell others what to do, even the shy waft of electricity that moves through someone's being as a response to merely being alive. Think of the millions who, throughout human history (there is no other) have always known what art is for, and have unquenchably gone on opining, Treischnitting and Kolberhoffing to their hearts', and bias's, content. One Frau T. or K. would have served for both of them, and indeed perhaps they shared the same woman as they marauded the same art. Can they be behind the foul campaign that slanders me in doggerel? I cannot say with certainty that I will not run into Treischnitt and Kolberhoff again, although if I were to I would take them on fully as I never did, querying the basis of all they did, *were* I to have them on my plate again, not allowing myself to be distracted by how fast they managed to walk in the park, as if to leave me and my cavil behind while they walked so hygienically ahead. I would take them on, I tell myself, as if I were not talking to Treischnitt and Kolberhoff at all, but to disgusting effigies with no power to reply, only the option of walking away northward toward the lake. After them I would go, with my shorter legs, hailing and catcalling them until they broke into a run, not as if I were pursuing Treischnitt and Kolberhoff at all, but circus versions of them, minus their trappings and reputation, until they threw themselves into the lake crying Behold what has become of him, whom we did our best to smooth down

101

back into the lower orders, now returned to threaten and abuse us. And the deaths they had, such as Treischnitt's, he gone first, would not be the deaths I let them have; I would drown them, say, lashed head to toe, or walk them silly through a series of tiger cages, they the former proud possessors of that unpossessable miracle: art. Thus my belated frenzy, conjured up in a dream of old Vienna, postcards and pretty corners, all small tables out in the breeze swathed in white cloths extending to the ground, and brought out fully clad by waiters who set them down reverently, with even the little candlelamps and ashtrays in place as if they have stolen an anthology from another form of life, they bear them outside like fully functioning trophies snatched from the mainstream of some other going-on. I remain awed by such confidence, having always thought the waiters would assemble the tables *after* having anchored them securely in place, as if for the evening service, fishing out from pouches in their smocks the needed implements: knives and forks, spoons, napkins, ashtrays, the small heartening-to-distant-travelers lamp. That is what it is to idealize something you have watched on countless evenings without ever having taken part, neither interloper nor invitee, neither waiter nor loiterer, not even for a final cigarette over a schnaps while the whole civilization wheeled about you like a constellation in the sky. That kind of voluptuous absenteeism can destroy your afterlife and rid you of all nostalgia, refining the idea, I suppose, until it alters from being a longing to have been there into something else: the longing not to long to have been there, abandonment of carefree *Sehnsucht,* my hearties, which means longing. How few of us, denied what we longed after, have achieved that mind-saving nullity of no longer wanting what we never had: reverse nostalgia I have come to call it, out of which one's more recent life has been made, and not by artisans or artificers, but by those inveterate benchmen, disappointment and failure. Never to look back even in the throes of yearning, so that yearning becomes a naked sense applicable to nothing you remember, but burning you still, where once it gave you a light surface scar, now sinking deep into the site and causing blood to flow you never knew you had. Those mantled tables arrayed in the dusk, set out for my enemies and despisers, should have blown away by now, like great works of art, but they do not, they linger, a constant invitation that has floated down from another, more polite planet, merely to get me going again, and the waiters have become robots, there is never food or drink, but all the motions of an apéritif taken, a guest welcomed, a breeze warded off, a mouth mopped with a crisp napkin of Irish linen, a cigarette already lit that will not go out and has been glowing since Alexander the Great. Oh, nostalgia, thou hast done me in, providing me with ghosts but ridding me quite of aesthetics, so that I end up a mild appreciator of minor social phenomena, as if at the beginning of an entirely new life. What a ravishing thought: I start over, a child but full-grown, allowed to seat myself at such tables even if denied fodder, with all around me the scions of the élite, nodding amiably to me as if they know my work and on the quiet have been buying it. Yes, that's him. Doesn't he look wonderful, so humble and grateful, asking nothing of anybody, he might be a carter or a drayman, pausing only to let the perspiration settle. If that is nostalgia then I am its muse. Of course, no such thing happens, not even in phantom form in the frail arena of my head. Made of words, I suppose, it hovers like a mirage and fades away as vapor, leaving behind its only exponent, he who owns the night and can remember only Frau Röntgen and her spouse's rays. Odd what survives, comes leaking through in tattered form, not as if you were remembering, but dismembering, and you all of a sudden recognize that you are not permitted to remember in a cogent, logical fashion, but have to continue with the merest motley of leftovers, vainly trying to link them up into a flawless record of a life lived. All you learn from this exercise in piecemeal hopefulness is how to utter something shorter than you wish it were, saying nothing fully because you do not want to be saying it at all: decorous abbreviation, or something such, something between fond loathing and tender impatience. I no sooner start something than I lose its thread, as if I am being penalized. Is this the promised penal colony? Am I Dreyfus? Dreyfusard? Can this be Devil's Island with only a grating for a roof, and the mindless sun beating down at me whereas I had always thought of hell as coming at you from beneath. Perhaps I am a black, brought here to be blanched by X-ray, as they used to do in the old days. Change my spots in the presence of raucous guards who pretend to set out those same small tables in the courtyard surrounded by barbed wire. I never get to join them, they who sit out there with rifles at the ready, evening strollers who sip and sip, languorously extend their legs as the slight eight o'clock tropic zephyr starts up, coming in from—where? Wherever it is cool. Are they my friends? Do they even know who I was? Have they ever heard of Vienna and an artist's tribulations there with Treischnitt and Kolberhoff? Do I have privileges after all? I am told I am allowed to change the dream, marry Treischnitt and Kolberhoff to Frau Röntgen in this whirligig of wanting, not that I cared, I just do not want either of them to have the basis of a future life. Then I will not be Dreyfus, I am

not that innocent, I mean I am not innocent to that degree, no cannot be. Yet what are these abundant flakes he
kicks his way through, wandering about his Lilliput of a
cell (the grating above, through which it never rains)? Has
he been woodworking to his thumbs' content? Are these
the petals of seaflowers blown in, the well-known marine
violet or the exquisite mandevilla dropping its trophies?
Wrong color: these flakes have a greenish hue, and he re-
alizes at long last, he who has been here long enough to
see whole generations of guards arrive and die off, with
scarcely a word said between them and him, that these are
his droppings, not in the vilest sense, but this is what happens when a man picks his nose for a whole life sentence,
letting the flakes fall where they will, not rolling them
into little projects to flick through the grating. Hygienic
thought, part of his sentence being the obligation to snite:
not a single handkerchief in never mind how many years,
but he long ago deceived himself that these were faint
petals blowing in from the distant strand, my hearties,
shreds of, oh he makes it up as he goes, that wholly unknown flower the *puella aurea,* the golden girl of the tide-
pools, born to soothe. Thus made to relax, I would like to
start the University of Devil's Island, not the most salu-
brious place to undertake studies of any kind, but à la

manière de Treischnitt and Kolberhoff, and none of those academics would be able to resist getting their hands on it, coming all that way to give free lectures because they cannot resist, they have to have power over everything, look after their own, which is tantamount to everything. In no time the cruise ships would be dropping the Herr Doktor Professors off so that they could compete for the Dreyfus Prize, the award half a ton of nose-flakes, the criteria unpublished, it all being up to the founder, I myself, whose whims—well, leave it at that. If we cannot have Fisher King Fellowships, then we can have Dreyfus Prizewinners, who will then go home and become cabinet ministers, geniuses of the doormat. Am I allowed to amend this dream? Heads of the Republic. Actually, this is not a bad place to belong to (as they say in the local pidgin translated: *me belonga Debil*), provided you don't stare too much at the ocean and steel yourself to contemplate the woof and texture of where you are, attending to every tiny facet as it hits you. No mental roaming unless you have a gift for coming back, to the scratched tin plates, the wooden spoons, the guillotine in the other courtyard, the beheaded pigs upon whom they practice for effect. If you can bear these folkways of our local university, then you are in at last. My first course, taught perhaps to the strains of Brahms, will be devoted to Hermann Hesse's *Under the Wheel,* book published as I arrived in Vienna for the second time and rather skimped as if I already knew what he was saying, but in retrospect definitive prophecy. The only way of getting a passing grade would be to go out into the world and make a total balls-up of your life for the sake of art. Then you might have a chance, especially if your reading of Hesse has led you on to Musil and the rest, those ace recommenders of rootless juvenility self-sacrificed to art. I mean Art. The trouble is: books. They do not encourage such things here, but you are allowed, ha, to dote on books you might have memorized before being assigned to the island. This makes of you a naturalist reader, minutely observing rocks, ants, roaches, birds and even guards as if they were sentences by Hesse, Musil, and the others, and it almost works, especially if you see these against the background of the teeming jungle in which, if you escape, you will smother, there is no different word for it. Here you may call any guard Treischnitt or Kolberhoff and thus exact a completely invisible vengeance just thinking of all that their sojourn here denies them. The real Treischnitt (ghost) and Kolberhoff are certain to show up here soon in order to compete for the Dreyfus Prize, little that they know of it: their hunger for medals et cetera knows no bounds, there is scarcely a place on their chests to pin anything new, no matter how august. Was becomes is. Is becomes was. All is in flux. On the boisterous sea breezes, ordinary air in a highly agitated state, there comes the fragrant aftermath of many a sublime conversation with Treischnitt and Kolberhoff, like some poignant sample of yet another island, all pineapple and frangipani, aromas to die for, re-sweetened by memories of their incessant endearments even while telling me about something mundane, the tightness of a shoe or the stiffness of a buttonhole in a lapel, resisting somewhat the insertion of yet another boutonnière saying what a wonderful fellow was wearing it, just like a bit of heaven sent in an envelope with a cardboard armature within to prevent it from bending or being crushed. My dearest fellow, my most august sir, were the overtures that began it, encouraging me to think—well, never mind, and readily followed up by, either Treischnitt or Kolberhoff, sometimes speaking as I have already said in ecstatic simultaneous fusion, Our beloved Fellow, Dearest chap, Our only hope, with the upper-case letters creeping gradually into the front of the words uttered as if the words themselves were to be regarded as titles: Our Beloved Fellow, Dearest Chap, Our Only Hope, all of this giving me the keenest sense that I had been elected, chosen, the only sample of my kind, I no sooner soaking up the one salutation than having to stomach another, which makes you wonder about hyperbole in the vocative: how many darlings can suitably follow a beloved? I mean, if you have been surfeited with the latter, how can they later demote you to darling or Darling Boy? It was all bewildering, yet not more so than when these words and phrases wafted in on dulcet evening breezes full of heavenly perfume and divine juices. In my mind they lined up in echelon, as on a ladder to paradise, I doing the ranking, not Treischnitt or Kolberhoff, who of course ejaculated the words not always in exact unison, clearly infatuated with my presence, yet each going his own way in the tribute. So I often responded, hugely, to a Darling out of place only to find a Dear Fellow following it, quite a demotion, but also vice versa, rising on the mediocre cloud of a Dear Fellow (or a Dearest Chap) to the full paean of a Darling Lad. You had to keep your wits about you during these interviews, while they looked at my newest work, even a postcard draft, and exclaimed in effusive phrases, suggesting I was The Find, the only one to start the Renaissance of Viennese art (and the superlative use of the capital letter already installed in the language for nouns). Indeed, as I look back on those palmy days, I recognize that I was responding to something more than the mere shift upward of attention you get when a Noun appears, I was receiving an intonation that the language registers only in phrasings, never in a single word unless you cap it with an evaluative formula such as *with tremulous awe* or *dribbling with acute regard* even as I uttered the word. To couch this in modern terms; no I will not couch anything. It is like when you write something down only to deny someone the pleasure of your voice, as crude as that. So, as I was saying, it became difficult to cope with their sublime endearments in fast flow in the presence of their banal subject matter (the shoe, the buttonhole), but not as difficult, for me anyway, as assimilating and preserving all the abundant good will in the context of their simultaneous indifference. It was all rhetoric, chunter, sporadic mouthing-off, with little behind it save a Viennese addiction to the cream cakes of discourse. You see my dilemma. How take them seriously, at their most lauding, when all the time I knew they were just oiling the machinery of their own aloofness. I was merely their foil. So it was bad enough to tolerate the Treischnitt-Kolberhoff blather, empty and fulsome, but not as hard and noxious as having to fend off the memory of so much involuntary adoration blown in on the tropic winds from lovelier islands than mine own. Ah, the disappointment, when their Dearests and Most Beloveds palled, and all I was left with was a Viennese intention, to lull the poor bastard's overdeveloped sense of

111

self-worth until he behaved like any normal frustrated human, reconciled to his lowly station, buoyed up by rhetoric but dragged down by realism. Even worse, when for once they shifted from endearment to anecdote and told me in full, Treischnitt and Kolberhoff narrating in full cry about the details of their Alpine marchings, and the hazards out there on the slippery slopes, always Treischnitt in the lead of course, but the feebler of the pair, planting his foot in the loam or schist, yet not moving forward, just working his mountaineering boot into the stuff to make a cavity, a slot, into which his boot would fit without slobbing sideways or forward, thus causing the human equivalent of a landslide. Many a whoa and steady now accompanied this maneuver of his, as it would with the vast Alps ahead, beside, behind, below, above them, they the merest speck on that superlative inhuman scape. The right trench had to be dug by the lead foot before an advance could be made, the real truth of the matter becoming, as I at last gathered, that they were never alone up there but accompanied by a small boy, maybe a shrunken youth, who assisted them, who had a keen eye for a gap in the loam or schist and would give his life to firm it up or make it deeper, always uttering his professional cry of Down we go, Herr Treischnitt and Herr Kolberhoff! This was when he came out with his Swiss Army knife, per-

haps his Austrian Army knife, and applied the pipe-
scraper flange to the sides of the slot, sometimes in what
seemed emergencies mixing up a little plaster of Paris
with spit to make a firm flank, even while Treischnitt and
Kolberhoff, those ace flatterers and lousy mountaineers,
cried out phrases of encouragement borrowed from who
knew what childhood reading: Bravo, young helpling,
What a doughty helpmeet, Oh for a thousand like him! It
made you sick to hear them recap all this, dialogue by dialogue, with the apple of their eye, the *Apfel* of their *Au-
gen,* young Egbert Schlöch, hovering beneath them always at the kneel, his kneecaps worn away by Alpine
service to these two old codgers who should never have
left the Ringstrasse but did so only out of dandyish
bravado. Had they been exclaiming, in extremis, even
while working to help Treischnitt to his second footfall in
that thin air, Bravo, Young Helpling! apropos of me, I
would have felt better about things, but they were not,
and neither are they doing so in memory blown in on the
seabreeze from Borneo or Australia, wherever *they* are. I
have to stiffen my resolve even to tolerate the image of
Egbert Schlöch at the kneel with Swiss Army knife dig-
ging at the welt-trough to help them go to a second step
at a speed of, I have now calculated, a yard an hour, or, far
less than the speed of human peristalsis. Had I been with

113

them—no, no more of that. I would have been able to get them up to saliva-spilling speed, or the velocity of blood from a slashed wrist. You have to try, and Egbert Schlöch was always playing for time, being paid by the hour. How they ever surmounted an Alp I never knew, but they always came back to serious thought with tales of deep-breasted, tanned Alpine girls wandering alone up there, rudely swyved by these two hearty rapists, once they had gotten under way and Egbert S. had fallen in behind them like a true retainer. One shove and all would have been well, but such was not their modus, they had to inch their way forward while dreaming up lies to regale me with, I who held the fort back in Vienna, Fort Austria as I sometimes called it. There were limits and Treischnitt and Kolberhoff had gone nowhere near them. Their world was all words, fake and fancy, while such as I groveling and pleading lived the life of the real, snubbed by the cafés, ousted by the shops, derided by the elegant women of fashion, spat upon by the men of fashion, always Moved On by the police, one branch of which actually moved the others on, and came into being for precisely that purpose, locally defined as the Other-Police-Force-Movers-On Brigade (Column A, under 21), which was a mouthful but not more so than the sight of them converging fifty strong on one solitary constable who had been too long in one place. Urging him forward, they established a model for Treischnitt and Kolberhoff, did they but know it, paying homage to mere motion, although on the level, to be sure. Watching all this while my two mentor-tormentors were up there mountaineering (fountaineering I called it), was painful, but I endured and did my best to put a manly face on things. Easier said than done, my dears (you don't mind if I Treischnitt and Kolberhoff you a little, do you? I have almost lost the habit of the spontaneous endearment). I am dealing with my *bête noire* again, Kolberhoff, who says extraordinary things to me, from you were dreaming, dearest fellow, to *Schwarmerei, Traumerei*, you wonderful chap. Of course, Treischnitt is no longer with us, which somehow makes Kolberhoff look taller, an impression that immediately brings Treischnitt back through the analogy of mere length. But, imagined back, in mind's eye, he shortens Kolberhoff again. It is hard to keep up with these shifting sizes, and I cannot decide how to ban the perished Treischnitt from my bank of memories. How oust him from the arena of potential good will when you, out of habit, still expect the best of him, them both? It's an old problem, most of all when you have had nothing from them and your sense of obligation to them rests on nothing as yet done on their part. You wither under a surfeit of expectation, a

115

birthday boy whose birthday never comes around. There
are some people who—shall I finish it? I will. Who want
the power without the least manifestation of taste, who
fancy themselves emperors of arts without knowing the
difference between gorgeous perspective and a rat's turd.
It's military in a way. They want to be conquerors and
ride in procession like ancient Romans, extolled and
revered for having interfered with millions of otherwise
peaceful, productive lives. The problem remains of
whether to look up to Kolberhoff because Treischnitt is
no longer there or look down on him because the Treischnitt image hangs on. I will never settle this muddle, all
the time of course hoping for my ship to come in, my
long desired Fisher King Fellowship to either Oxford or
Cambridge, to dine there with port and walnuts, or to
some other haunt of art such as Paris. I am not proud,
willing to go wherever sent. I mention this to the afore-
said heightened/shrunken Kolberhoff, but he scoffs at the
very idea. Darling man, he cries, there is no such thing as
a Fisher King Fellowship, there never was. Didn't Treischnitt ever tell you, it was a dream we fudged up to get
people groveling in front of us, to see how much they really wanted that kind of thing. We may have had such
things ourselves back in the good old days, but not now,
there is no money, the country is spent up. Were you truly

expecting it? Well, we must do something for you, far nobler than that. I was suspicious, though: once bitten, twice bitten. And who was this we? The aggregation of all people such as he, the living and the dead, or some secret group I'd never heard of? I could tell he was in no mood to be trifled with by a purveyor of postcards, not while he was grieving about Treischnitt, the taller, and constantly bringing him to mind in talk, as if to conjure up the old synod merely to bamboozle the likes of me. I was learning, though: the presence of the dead and gone affected profoundly the way you saw the living, almost as if you now saw everything through a kaleidoscope, new with every shake. The Treischnitts had uncanny power, stronger presences where recalled than when present. In a way, this was merely to say nothing had changed, but my reasoning took me a stage further, something like this: If these two worthies had exerted a dead hand on the tiller of the future's art, then one of them dead increased their power over us. They were deader than they had been before, deader even than then. I began to see how a couple of corpses named Treischnitt and Kolberhoff could have accomplished all they did without the least effort: a dead weight was the only thing required, just to keep the rising generation in its place, just to hold the backlash back, to keep mongrels such as me in their hovels, peering at free

117

newspapers, too badly dressed to go out and gape at the
Terza Rima, though I often did, the pariah of dusk. There
was another element in this equation too: money. Little as
they thrilled to art, especially its spiritual side, growling
Traumerei, Schwarmerei, they wanted money even more,
recognizing wealth and wealth only as the true badge of
success so that, say, having laid one rug in a room, they
laid another on top of it, and so on, until they wallowed
in several. Conspicuous consumption. If I ever had my
way, I would roll them up in those rugs and slide them
into the Baltic or some lake. You may well conclude I had
been living in a fool's paradise (fools are addicted to paradise, *meine Herren*), waiting for my Fisher King to come
through, perhaps an actual king like one riding in triumph through Persepolis. That would have been Tamer-
lane the Great would it not? Never mind. I longed for
some recognition, salivated for help, little realizing how all
the help went the other way, to those who already had,
thus revealing them as multiple ikons of success. I had
never thought about success, of course, wanting only the
spiritual affinity of the eager appreciator confronted with
the inexhaustible object of contemplation. What a luscious mouthful. So there was going to be no Fellowship,
even though in his hypocrite's way Kolberhoff blathered
about a special "dispensation" being arranged for me, a

Destiny he called it, clearly an arrangement between Kolberhoff and Treischnitt before Treischnitt died. Could it
be that the source of largesse had been Treischnitt all
along, curbed by the penny-pinching Kolberhoff, who
now had free range over Frau Treischnitt-Kolberhoff (I
had long assumed she was a joint property, one woman
for both men). Had she ever walked with them in the
Alps, getting her footmarks plastered hard by the egre-
gious Egbert Schlöch? These were fighting thoughts I
tried to fend off while guessing at the special dispensation, the pearly appointment I was destined for. Once a
sucker, always. I could not quell the part of me that ever
hoped. Perhaps such was the racial memory, inescapable,
and the desire the fused voices of my questing ancestors
heard as in a seashell. What was this marvel he refused to
unveil? I spoke of my postcards, but Kolberhoff, the Trei-
schnitt-less Kolberhoff, waved my questions away, babbling about the delight of surprise, admitting only that it
would not be in Vienna, and at once my hopes revived of
autumn, say, among my beloved English: punts on the
Cam or Isis, May mornings celebrated with roses and
blushing lasses, the still, dank quiet of libraries musty with
old thought. No more Viennese cafés for me. I could see
it now, old me scurrying around the colleges with crusts
of bread in the long pockets of my jet-black gown. Not

119

an artist's dream at all, you may observe, but I would be peacefully at work on the Queue-Tee, not far from London. I therefore took his word for it and stopped worrying, knowing that, if he had something in store for me then he wasn't the lying oaf I'd thought him even when he was with Treischnitt. Life so far, I thought, had been a toss-up, always a prank between poverty and novelty. I wanted to settle down and be a credit to my parents. Dearest fellow, he said, now I see I have got you looking forward, as in the old days of Kolberhoff and Treischnitt, when we had all those stimulating conversations about art and perspective. *Ja.* Strange how, when one's dearest companion dies, one loses interest in perspective, as if the world has become two-dimensional. It is the receding-narrowing one wishes to be rid of, if you see, my sweet. I was far from being the sweet of this pretentious dabbler of a moneybags who had eased his way into power because he was well-to-do, but knew nothing of late nineteenth-century painting, say, or even of architecture in general. He was a broker, like the rest of them, a Nero of good will, now doubly crass trying to compensate for the loss of Treischnitt; he had to be Treischnitt as well now, both a tall and a short man, both an altruist and a dreamer. He would never make it, I could tell, the strain was deep within him and he would never head for the deep-

120

breasted tanned girls in the Alps again, nor require the footprint services of Egbert Schlöch, who had no doubt already moved on to other mountaineers with even bigger, stodgier feet. His quizzical squinny always made me nervous, even more so now as as he seemed to anticipate my stupid answer, already forming his lips into the rictus of contempt as my muddled brain fumbled for a reply. My talk with him had always been a mess, I never knowing how to answer because mesmerized by (a) too many empty endearments, (b) so much vague and abstract stuff about the miracles they were going to work for me, always cast—Treischnitt or Kolberhoff—in cheerful tropes such as the august resonance of your breakthrough, the *réclame* due to you from all and sundry, the sheer joy of work accomplished. They had always fattened their talk with empty phrases, unable to resist, say, an *all and sundry* or *as long as we have art.* That sort of intellectual farting you get to know if you talk much with bureaucrats: not the keen, but diffused almost hospitable aroma of certain flatuses, but the overripe, highly active, arsenical green fart from deep within the body processes, evoking dead donkey or year-old fish. That was the cigar-mellowed aroma of these darling fellows. I had even tried to reciprocate his endearments—theirs—but Kolberhoff had glared, sneered, and waved me away to the Terza Rima or wherever. You just

121

did not address him in such terms. He always insisted on his full array of titles, which life is too short for me to reproduce, although the word *Kunst* uncannily occurred more than once, as if this dodo knew anything of art. A penguin knew more of Dante than he did of pain. Nor could I call him Kolberhoff to his face, and certainly not Hans, a name only Treischnitt was allowed to use, and he not often. His initials were J.R.P. K.N., but what they stood for I had no idea. Joachim Rolf Pieter Klaus— what could N stand for? Perhaps it was just an N, its underside hiding the slug of nihilism perhaps. So he was the Herr Doktor Professor Künstler of something or other, in some eyes a shrunken Chinaman with a face like a badly designed potato, all knobs and "eyes," with a fair helping of warts above his eyebrows. It was a face of incalculable wear. I do not add tear because that is just what *he* would have done.

Does not a man see his own face

DOES NOT A MAN SEE HIS OWN FACE more keenly when a friend has just died? Or never sees himself again, in his ears echoing that dreadful goodbye: we will never see each other again. I began to see in Kolberhoff's face how he saw himself, continually examining himself as if puzzled he had survived. His mangled grace. The unformed cravings that would never develop, not now. The way he had of smiling without opening his mouth, when the cares of life become the caress of fate. His sudden access of command. The tiny click his lips made when he *did* part them. The heroic agreeableness that comes after the spirit has almost been broken and he finds himself on the terminal moraine of surrender. Those heavy-lidded eyes now have enough to conceal whereas previously they bounced about with too little to do. Now he watches fatality even in the eyes of children, murmuring. A teacher affects eternity, it is bound to be so. The muscles above his nose have tensed his brow into a series of vertical lines, but now he has a

trio of horizontal ones that come from agitated wrin-
kling. He is getting on in the bad sense. The trouble with
life is that, by the time you have made something of yourself, those you want to be proud of you have left the
scene. An ailing bee in autumn, he was with uneven, frag-
ile steps, walking the same wavy line as the famed Swan
of Tuonela, forever sidling between life and death. He
murmurs the Latin word *interfecit,* meaning "he killed,"
while imagining himself a *paropemassis,* a mountain
around which eagles dare not fly. He has by-passed the
gluttony of the self-engrossed, grafting it all on to that
somber voice of his. His eyes water constantly perhaps because the same gold fleck has entered them that one sees
in the weave of his trews, or is it some baleful entity
twirling away at the fringe of his vision, daring him to
hope never again to be affected by cold, wind, heat, sun,
pain, or radioactivity? Or perhaps it is only the smoke he
has always managed to puff away from his eyes, and now
it is all coming back for revenge, caught as he always is between angelic impulses and predatory lusts, saying those
who do not live life will be dominated by it. He has done
his best, he sees that in his punished features. Wishes he
had grown taller with experience, whereas in fact he has
shortened. His old friend Treischnitt is only just around
the corner. So he thinks, construing that assumption in

the worst sense, but he may just be lucky enough, he
hopes, to live another twenty, thirty, years, not so much to
accomplish anything as to deny the gods who would love
to get him by the short hairs. And twist. Has he done
enough? For whom? He looks back along a huge pas-
sageway of philanthropy, altruism, unaware of the power
he acquired, trampling friends. He still flashes his cuffs
and their golden links, smoothes the outline of his silver
hair, sometimes burrowing into space where hair used to
be and stopping short. His head was on the move. His
forehead sloped back at a dizzying rate as if it had been
scooped rearward while still molten and a huge, deep
crease shaped like an S ran all the way from his nose to the
underside of his chin. The entire face had a punished,
squashed, roughed-up texture. Who knew what he had
been through? Treischnitt, for all his tallness, had had the
cuddlier face of the two, cute with assorted cheery wiles,
an eye twinkle and a preternatural readiness to smile,
which of course meant only that behind the smile he
conducted his most secret activities. The hard taskmaster
that Kolberhoff was, his face displayed, and his very bearing, histrionically sloped head canted far back as if to
achieve the perfect demeanor: aloofness and invulnerabil-
ity in one. It was hardly the face of a giver, a catalyst, not
one from whom you could expect bounty or guidance,

but rather a call to order, an instruction to brace up and get on with things, leaving him alone to get on with matters more serious. It was therefore amazing that he took any interest in me at all, categorical and stiff as it was, hoping to shed me rather than launch me. All the stranger, then, that in his brusque way he told me he had come up with something for me that would appeal to my exotic tastes, to the wanderer in me, the exile. Could this be his way of saying Oxford, Cambridge, London even? The only snag, I knew, was the impending war, with the atmosphere of Vienna, maybe even Austria and Europe, sultry and oppressive as it was before a thunderstorm, with people becoming more and more irritable, not so much tempers fraying as tightening, and sleep becoming difficult. Something was going to happen, and it would bring to a halt all kinds of international exchange: the demise of fellowship and Fellowships, I thought; but Kolberhoff had come up with something, perhaps delving into the darkest recesses of bureaucracy to find a way through, something little known, an exception that might just weather the blast when it came, even if England were involved. I could see that it would be hard for any European country to abstain: they all had war on their minds, and it would spill over into Africa even and the Middle East. This was a poor time to be looking for favors, especially the kind an

128

artist desires. I mean, who fondles art during a national crisis? He seemed pleased with himself, however, although reluctant to embark on the speech that would crack the mystery wide open. His manner was almost sexual, his overture very nearly coy, as he proffered the not very fat packet that enclosed the good news of my Fisher King, or whatever. You will enjoy this, he said, perhaps not exactly the thing you were looking forward to, but it has all the right elements: foreign, of lengthy duration, all provided, and plenty of spare time. Good, convivial company. I could see myself swigging port and cracking walnuts even now. Well, if not that, what? He still would not open up, but brandished the brown envelope like a wand before me, lapsing into his old endearments from Dear Fellow to Darling Man, gushing to the maximum, actually reaching forward with his head still tilted back as if to look over me and patting my arm where I stood, he, Kolberhoff, not the taller of the pair, and it was as if the ghost of Treischnitt, the semi-cozy, stood there urging me to accept, wishing me all good fortune in my new endeavor, whatever it was. Clearly, the inspiration had been his, and the actual delivery something arranged between the pair of them long ago. All that was missing was his finesse, his finishing touch, for they were a couple of old roosters in their frock coats, more addicted to tight

129

little ceremonies than to anything enduringly construc-
tive. The new century had come and gone, Austria
patched together for too long had come apart where it
had been glued together, and Europe was boiling, almost
as if 1900 should have brought something momentous
with it that was now long overdue, not so much a work
of art as something political, and was just now coming to
it. Kolberhoff of course would not change, he was too set
in his ways, as well as too well entrenched in his appointment, unless he died, and even then he might endure as a
posthumous Fisher King. I feinted at the envelope with a
levity I did not feel, I had never made such a gesture before in that impersonal room, and Kolberhoff withdrew it
from my reach, wanting to hold on to it as long as possible and getting me to squirm. You will have to answer it,
he said, and sign yourself away. It has repercussions, but, as
we well know, you are free of the clutches of the Austrian
army, too feeble and infirm, et cetera, so we don't have
that to worry about. In a sense, then, you are a free man,
available. His voice rarely italicized since his chosen mode
of speech was monotonous; he loved not to give anything
away: no hint of favor or enthusiasm, but the same boxed
growl as if the steep slope of his brow had spoken. There
will be guidance, my dear, don't you worry about that,
and there will be no language problem. Oh? I had rather

looked forward to grappling with upper-class English, that dry, gobbling sound English was famous for. Oh well, come what may, I was going to ship out. First he fanned me with it. This was August, 1914; he meant well, it was stifling in that ornate office of his, even without Treischnitt whose bulk had displaced a certain amount of air. I was fast losing patience, now I knew it was not to be Cam-ward, Isis-ward, unless.... He opened the envelope, unfolded the documents, and pretended to begin to read, but he was improvising some jargon of his own, wasn't he, mainly numbers and categories used by the Fisher Kings of old and therefore lengthy, reaching back into the deepest nineteenth century. Henceforth, my bully boy, he told me, in spite of your being Austrian, you will serve as a newly appointed Fisher King emissary to the Sixteenth Bavarian Reserve Infantry Regiment, also known as the List Regiment. You are summoned to report. Your fondest wish has been granted, my good fellow. We hate to lose you, Kunst, but we cannot have everything, we cannot hold on to you for ever, can we now? Herr Doktor von Treischnitt would have been delighted. I imagine that, wherever he is, he is purring. All you are required to do is present yourself. He smiled, which was to say his face seemed to come apart. War had already been declared days earlier, and here I was, destined for Munich, into the thick of it, due for training and no doubt the Front. Thus ended my blossomy dreams of a quiet three years by the Isis and the Cam, dawdling in punts while pondering huge altar-pieces. No more postcards. Well, perhaps a few. I had been duped by an expert. Yet, trained like a seal, I said my thankyous and stumbled away, wondering how many other young Austrians had just been finagled into something they never dreamed of. If I was one at all, I was the last of the Fisher Kinglets, delivered up less to a country than to a language, just as others would be fighting for French or Hungarian. The international language of art had failed us, or perhaps not; it had simply never been used, because, well, people wanted to have a war, like changing from croquet to tennis. Now they would get one, and helpless youths such as I would get mixed up in it, all their bright tender ambitions shut away for later. Contrasted with that somber prospect, all my tidy visions of a beloved place in the mountains, say, with a view of ice reefs and muted flowers where the frail chamois prowled, slid away. You no sooner find your idyll than someone close to you says I don't care for that kind of accordion music, or I loathe the kind of boisterous sea breeze that tousles the napkins, or it's too quiet up there, I am not an eagle after all. So you come to the dismaying conclusion that, having found your perfect place to share with some beloved, you will be obliged to live in it alone, quietly to yourself extolling the sunsets there, the hugeness of the local bees, the region's unique wines. What is that old maxim? A pleasure shared is a pleasure doubled? Well, in my case it would always be halved, I would always have to be taking my own word for something, with never a sigh or gasp of assent from some other being. There was always pedantry about flora and fauna, local restaurants, local conversation, as if no one in the whole world save me could ever cleave to the heart of a place, not its trappings but its *Geist,* and thus allow the erring heart to rest itself a while in a flawless surrounding. For how long can music, even the best, do duty for conversation? I ask you. Or food for company? Constantly you hear the echo of your own conviction, vainly writing to former friends to come and share your paradise with you, but they have taxes to pay, lectures to give, reports to write, relatives to succor, friends to befriend or re-befriend. You stroll through the guest apartments, acquainting yourself with the inertia of emptiness, wondering how so and so would have looked in bed, or at the breakfast table, or halfway into his cups at midnight. The result is that you become a super-soul, doomed to an incessant diet of yourself even as you grow greater in the external world's regard, but a sheep of silence ever thickening its mountain wool as you, isolated

133

as a German Romantic poet, inspect the same old water-
fall, sinkhole, crag or broken gate, monarch of all you sur-
vey but, in a way, a splendid pariah in the end quite willing to bribe people to come share your marvels, applaud
your good taste, even a Treischnitt or a Kolberhoff, whose
unanswered invitations lay thick on the mantelpiece held
down by unopened tins of aromatic tobacco, shredded or
formed into a disc. Such is the career of the innovator,
perched in his eyrie or huddled in a lean-to among the
trenches, tuning in to the birds of prey or the next bom-
bardment. I had met people whose father had counseled
them to solace themselves, when lonely, with the warm
nutty smell of a briar pipe, toasty in the cup of the hand,
sizzling just a bit but an ally, a double, a henchman, but
that was not for me: no mechanical apparatus of joy or
comfort, but shall we say a live victim trapped there until
the next funicular or train? It would have been good to
have somebody willing I could work on. Why, there were
even life's born refusers (not refuse but those who constantly refused), claiming they could not leave without
their collection of binoculars, several suitcases' worth at
least, not to mention the extra lenses, lens-cloths, and
tripods required for inspecting a hitherto unseen place,
which would demand a few extra suitcases lined with velvet even for the journey to begin. But it was always worse

than that, with crumb-trays and fingerbowls invoked, antimacassars of a certain aroma (don't you mean anti-massacres, I'd say) and bedpans, footwarmers, mustache trimmers and pounds of wax. Do you not know, they'd cry, that the great Lord Byron, when he traveled in Europe, had coach upon coach of absolutely imperative things needed en route or at some vexing destination? He could not travel without taking his estate with him, and his retinue was vast. I, who had thought the matter one of briefcases, urns, books, and weathervanes, had a second think coming: Anyone who had settled anywhere just could not be moved, simply could not be uprooted and sent on his way with only a pipe, some Balkan Sobranie, and a Bible. There was no such beast, whereas I, whoever that is, could even contemplate writing my life story in a prison cell, supplied with soup and paper. I had come into the world to make it shed its trappings, to trim life to its essentials, but most of my fellow creatures were intent on loading themselves down with booty. Was that why, when I painted, I wrote my name in thick letters, legibly quite large, as if the name were the real theme of the painting? This way you could even sign houses. Perhaps the loveliest aspect of this mountain retreat would be not the tar-black lake lying beneath it in the valley, but the local shop, wherein a Schlöch would fold your newspaper exactly as you liked it: double, triple, quadruple, or already opened up to the sports or literary page and everythiing else folded back or away from the relevant column, as in a circumcision. Good old Schlöch, not quite limber enough to minister to footprints with plaster of Paris, he would never have to be spoken to; he knew what people smoked, fried in, crammed into their sandwiches. It was a wurst shop he ran, really, but also a post office redolent with ham on hooks and ancient cheeses off which, perhaps once a year, some unsuspecting visitor would buy a corner to gas himself with, vomiting into the ravine with all the locals, wiser by half, laughing at his discomfiture. It would be that kind of local knockabout, all jams and jellies, strudels and sausage, black bread and a special mustard with tiny shreds of children's golden hair mixed into it, the *Senft Goldilochs* we called it. Only locals got the joke, of course. Schlöch's masterpiece was a newspaper folded, after a week's effort, into a swastika shape, with much heaving and twisting and some slitting with a razor, but accomplished all the same and, in the end, elegantly suspended among the hams. It rotated like a star in the mountain breeze and kept us cheerful all winter. If you lived long enough, I thought, you gathered up some social anthropology: not capering savages with bones through their noses, but friends bidding you farewell as

136

you set out for your midwinter vacation in the sun, pleading for a jolly card of palm trees and pink sand, but actually hoping you would slip and drown, suffer a concussion
from a coconut or some terrible fish poisoning reserved
for tourists. It was always rash to tell them anything good
about your stay in the subtropics or on the Black Sea; better to say the sea was polluted with dead jellyfish, the sand
was full of fleas like the mattresses in the albergo de joie,
and the natives revolting. Prices high, bread stale, exchange rate ruinous if you could even find a bank open.
That sort of thing was worth preserving, if not in a scrap-
book, then in a little silver ampoule in the brain. In the
end it was better to vacation in a miserable place, all snow
and gales and leather soup, then there was nothing good
to conceal and you did not risk losing friends merely for
having a good time. Perhaps they would even come to see
you in your mountain lair, when you could don your special white and gold tunic for them and strut along the
parapet as when in Paris, et cetera. No matter how well
you prosper in this life, you have to heed what you came
from and always keep a hole in your shoe. We were all
Schlöchs to begin with, he who also officiates at the
neighborhood inn, the Trout, where guests have to purchase the little carved wooden knives, forks and spoons he
offers them. Without them, eat with hands, or the one

137

you keep cleanest. Most buy but leave the cutlery behind, which he re-sells. He is doing all right for a clog-print-firmer-upper, a bit here, a lot there, his nostrils taking the form of a clean-cut right angle, appallingly ugly really, though I have heard it said this feature is very lascivious-looking in actresses. Schlöch has learned, and passed on, the way to deal with visitors: with Americans, just keep saying "Waal, ah'm all set," and everything is forgiven, as by the French if you keep saying *soi-disant,* a phrase that calls the whole world into question, and by the so-correct English (who hate being called the British) if you keep muttering the vital words such as "Balliol" and "Mag-dalen," interspersing these little outbursts with the word "Extraordinary," said slowly and split up by syllable with colossal emphasis on the OR bit: ex-TROR-dnry. This much is easy, even if you happen to be the former cham-pagne salesman Ribbentrop bamboozling the sheep as he curtseys them to the slaughter. It is true, for Treischnitt as for Kolberhoff, if you can't get the world to come and join you in Vienna or up the mountain, occupy it, take it over, bring them all into the fold and then forcefeed them with unsugared oatmeal. Was I not dreaming? Going too far forward, with famous aviators from several countries parading on the balcony with me, members of the British royal family confiding that I had all that it took, eminent

Italians and Hungarians and even the skulking Japanese, all come to pay homage to a copier of postcards, as if I were an antique show in my own right. It takes courage to rise so far above your station that you suffer from hypoxia, but you have to reach for the skies (*vide* Treischnitt of course), like the legless air ace Mister Bader. Was he not the one who, legless, asked to have his right arm cut off and sent home to London, then his left? The commandant said to him, "Squadron Leader, you are trying to escape." All such men bowing to the core of Vienna, to the courage of taking it on, tackling it, Kolberhoff-like and Treischnitt-like, until it succumbed and I was in demand. Fancy another country demanding that I help out! Imagine the war without me, which would not have been half so interesting, or decisive in scope. You can have a war without Treischnitts and Kolberhoffs, though let it be said that most wars are in fact fought on behalf of the Treischnitts and Kolberhoffs, dead or alive, hovering behind to record it all aright, in illuminated letters like medieval monks. It is comforting to look back on what turned out to be one's pre-destiny, an aberration, really, a dry run of no career value even while all the vital hordes were massing nearby. So, someone troops the colors and you get called to them; almost any flag will do, as long as it ropes in Köbel, Steinitz, and Probstschule, but not, of course,

139

Klarf, Ulruhst and Delbers. They take Kolnsheft but not
Döbelzeiss, as well as Klötzheide, Funknasch, and Zwölftraum, overlooking both Errol von Knechtvold and
Joachim Kerbsvogler, but not Grenzhaus and Plöchnasch.
Klaus, Odel, and Pfintner, yet omitting for unknown reasons Fnenck, von Traub, von Eschpitz, Dünckner, and
Klemp, who may all for all I knew have signed up for
Austria rather than being press ganged for Germany. But
you could not snatch a Poleisterman and a Kleister without also helping yourself to a Prinzlamp or a Dohnanyi,
so off they went as well, at least one of us astounded by
the frequency with which the truly Austrian name Pro-
haska seemed to show up, as if all of them had just sprung
fully formed for military duty from the nether lips of
their mothers. The main thing was that, one way or another, we would all be in it together, like maggots infest-
ing a corpse. And the corpse? Jolly old Europe, ready for
the last rot, and not *rot* for *red,* but rot for uncontrolled
putrefaction. Would they, I wondered, even call up the
colors to the colors, alizarin and sienna and arsenical
green? It would make sense would it not? Thank God for
a change of scene, of venue, a new style of poverty, of luxury even. A sense of purpose not seen since the Ancient
Athenians ran the polis hummed through our ranks. One
image, out of the thousands that came to delight me in

later times (not *that* much later), came from Hollywood movies, of which I preferred the cheerful, songful type. Nothing *noir* for the likes of me. This is not to say that my favorite image appeared only in movies I enjoyed. Not so. It appeared all the time, and it was the unusual way American actors, and therefore presumably American people in general, dealt with the telephone, not just picking up the receiver but also lifting the cradle by sliding at least two fingers into the slot and actually carrying the telephone to where they wished to sit, or walking about the room while holding the whole apparatus! This always struck me as a powerful move, revealing a disinclination to be tethered, as by the Treischnitts or the Kolberhoffs, say, and I thought: This is what it is like to have the world in one's grasp, the entire world, carrying it to where it was most convenient to have it, making it answer one's bidding, making a portable model of it whereas in other countries people felt obliged to stay where the phone was plugged in. I saw that Americans had endless lengths of cable to roam about with, looping and folding it to suit their convenience, even walking into another room, the bathroom perhaps, while continuing to talk. Here was a human specimen unconstrained by an appliance, and that appliance was the world, the whole world of talk in little! I never got over this apparition, which taught me how one

141

should deal with Earth and machines, grist for our mill. How come someone too weak and incapable, as the record said, to fight for Austria had been conscripted for Germany, with help from the Kolberhoffs? Was this a swindle or the most cunning piece of altruism Europe had ever seen? I should have refused the envelope, thrown it back in his face with a Why aren't you volunteering, you old heap of bourgeois crap? He would have looked beyond me and said nothing, certain he had found the right counter to all my pleas, all that groveling and asking. I had been disposed of, sent packing, my occupation— Vienna Painter—already on the death warrant. Who expected to survive? If Austria would have been too much for my pathetic body, just imagine what Germany would do! Had someone from way back used an allusion of mine against me? I mean when I once spoke of the Artist's Rifles. This had been the clue; they had worked on me for the best result, and here it was. Unless they, Treischnitt and Kolberhoff, had a masterplan of devoting moral and physical weaklings to the German army in order to undermine it. Could they be that ingenious and potent? That clever. I doubted it. I could stay where I was and be safely left alone, exempted from war by beloved Austria. Or, in a mood of boredom and fatal curiosity, I could report for training, just to see how I got on. I could

142

always desert, could I not? Had Kolberhoff hit on the very thing I needed to snap me out of my visionary lethargy? After which I would go on to replace him at the Academy as both aesthete supremo and man of the world? This was not the last the world would hear of me. Here was the golden slipper, I urged myself, don it and go. There are risks, of course, and there be dragons. I will soon be someone else, my vignettes of military life will be famous, demanding perhaps transfer to the Artist's Rifles, no that would be the enemy, but they would hanker after me anyway, not to shoot, but to draw. When would I be free again? Was I free even now? Kolberhoff had pushed me at last out the door of his life, no doubt to deal with some other tyro, to be conned into accepting duty in Africa on Fisher King Fellowship AUS/AFR 19, whereas my own was AUS/DEU 1. I invented the figures, but they were no solace. Sallow narcissist that I was, I had no inkling of what I thought my fellowship life would be like. Probably much like the dreary life I lived in the hostels and boarding houses, cafés and beer halls, planning the timetable of my greatness. In a way, it was impossible to refuse Europe, to go up in smoke with it, and later to come down to earth again a fully qualified European, which I would not have been, skulking away in some Vienna garret until hostilities ceased. I little knew that I would soon be in Belgium amid a dreadful commotion, and writing letters to my former landlord, with feverish eyes among the ruined hedges and turnip fields. What was I? As ever, I was a courier. He who bites the bullet need not eat the gun.

Kolberhoff, Vienna 1945
for Treischnitt

Afterword

Afterword: A Trace of *Noir*

I feel impelled to add, not so much in vindication as in encouragement (for this is a text with a multiple personality), that while the events evoked—the Vienna of 1907–1914 —may prove to be one of history's cottages, the cottage did explode, devastating much of Europe. The effect I have sought may be akin to that of Greek tragedy, in which, as is commonly known, the events take place "off stage." They certainly do in *The Dry Danube*. No blood gets shed, though a sensitive reader can no doubt hear it drumming in the novella's vascular system, especially if Vienna, as may well be argued, was the microcosm of Europe at this time. Enough, I think, has been done with and said about the horrors of that long interrupted span of 1914 to 1945, perhaps not enough with the phoniness of such peace as there was, while the whole mess was boiling up behind scenes of benign good temper on the Serpentine, in the Bois de Boulogne and on the Riviera, out on the Wannsee, the eventual site of an evil conference about the extermination of Jews. My Kolberhoff, intruding himself beyond the ghost of *Anschluss* past, as it were, takes enormous liberties, but he is writing fiction after all, exploiting facts and fantasies to make a special point, exploring the queasy hinterland between vengeful embellishment and mesmerized echo. He cannot be blamed, at eighty-one and later perhaps yielding to a temptation to get it all down, off his chest, before it is too late. Obviously, the book, short enough, needs to be read twice for the double effect intended, for the reader to savor the warp between (in the first reading) a dawning suspicion as to who might be talking and (in the second) the certainty that this is a new personage in charge, perhaps unreliable, but efflorescing from the first presentation (with little Honeggerian hints to the alert reader about what is going on: Honegger's Piano Concertino dates from 1924, for example, and those little trotting horses on the keyboard may recall to mind Beethoven's Fifth as envisioned by E. M. Forster in *Howards End,* where the horses are goblins). The sedulous reader now has to check the date of that particular novel, just to see what Kolberhoff and I are up to.

Preparations for reading can be protracted endlessly, especially if a text arrives subtitled "A Forgery," with all that that *implies,* this being the art world in any case. What I had in mind throughout after some rather well-behaved "historical novels" (in one of which, however, Count von Stauffenberg narrates his own execution and then restages it), was a quizzical amalgam of torn paper and forgotten connections, much the kind of thing that happens to history as the world speeds up and the present displaces the past, foreshortening and mythicizing it until little remains save composite figures and slovenly synecdoches—parts doing duty for the whole as Nazis begin to fade into the image of the most heinous one, and Bormann's distraught wire to his wife, say, or Magda Goebbels's mercy-slaughter of her six children, disappear into the mirage of anecdote. In an age in which the movies peddle eugenics while pretending to be factual, history has to be eaten on the run: a true atavism this, since our ancestors did exactly that. One image that haunts and helps me is that of a war's discarded spears and banners dumped in a heap, a Roman image perhaps, my own special heap including documents and reputations, so much so that imaginary figures fall into the same rubbish-pile as genuine historical personages. Maybe no one cares, and the only viable role for a Kolberhoff, who writes his text without help from Treischnitt, is to wake us up briefly to certain preludes before the whole episode lapses again into oblivion. To be meddling with so many discarded images incites imagination, to be sure, and perhaps keeps fiction alive while its tried and true manifolds rot. I hope so. One presumes to interfere with a decay that is also a decadence, as W. H. Auden once indicated by stationing, in his rooms at Oxford, a rotten orange on the mantelpiece, bad side outward. Was this also Ezra Pound's old bitch gone in the teeth?

Obviously, Kolberhoff is a "loaded" narrator, knowing more than we do about events from 1918 to 1945, and knowing better. He leaves us wondering, I hope, which drove Hitler more: rage at his rejection by the art virtuosi of Vienna or the voluptuous rapture he got from music, especially Wagner's. Some infernal mix came together in his Vienna and army days and turned lethal soon after. We go on wondering, if we care at all in a world that has already transformed the hempen nooses in the Plötzensee execution shed into piano wire, thanks to some sloppy historians and heaven knows how many manipulative commentators. We wonder in the presence of myth obtusely yet traditionally made, and hold on to only a distinction that says myth is public fiction, fiction is a private one.

Trouble begins when the fiction writer or novelist feels obliged to use those piano-wire nooses instead of hempen ones because otherwise the image—of Nazi reprisal upon those who plotted against Hitler—lacks dramatic shock. A milder image that may indeed remain

150

as it more or less was is the planeload of ground pepper and twelve cases of condoms airlifted to freezing Nazi soldiers in the depths of the Russian winter. That image has teeth already, whereas, for reasons that elude me, hempen nooses do not. Perhaps the art-form we call fiction is merely tantric.

This is a novella perched on the brink of a grotesque hinterland that almost anyone with an inkling of history can supply. Of course, Kolberhoff's sense of that hinterland will not be the reader's, except by proxy (and not much of that because he too is suppressing, merely gesturing), but his awareness of it is bound to trigger that of the reader, who may become attuned during the actual reading or experience the shock of recognition and recall after the reading is over. In that sense, then, this book is a prelude or pendant, a dark reminder of how a seemingly innocuous person can fester into an ogre. Who is going to predict a demonic future for a young war hero (two Iron Crosses) with a passion for exalting music and matter-of-fact art? This overture to a rampage is perhaps more appalling than the rampage itself or the corrupt vision of the thousand-year Reich. Conceivably, one day, perhaps soon, perhaps not, when people have just about forgotten Hitler, this novella will have an eerie, ghostly quality, like a fabrication by a young saint and do-gooder, or at least one fabricated on his behalf. Who *was* this rather pallid visionary? What did he accomplish? Was he just another wannabe, barefoot on the track to nowhere? Reduced to bare essentials, the precareer of Winston Churchill looks far more threatening, and Roosevelt promises none too well.

I am left with a memory of how English poets of the Renaissance addressed themselves to what they called "the matter of Greece and of Rome," manhandling it as they saw fit as something malleable and exploitable. So we, gradually, with the matter of Nazi Germany (and surrounding countries). The enterprising reader may well wonder if Kolberhoff got to know the work of the Austrian novelist and playwright Thomas Bernhard. One doubts it and therefore attributes any Bernhardisms to the author as salutes and homages. What is perhaps just as clear is that Kolberhoff must have seen some of the miserable aftermath to World War Two from 1945 to 1955, in his eighties, a born survivor. It is doubtful that he attained the age of one hundred and thirty-six, but he may have made it to ninety (1955). In any event, writing in 1945 at eighty-one, he has already seen the worst, enough to provide him with countless examples of what the Ancient Athenians called *deinosis,* meaning something at its worst, which became the awful but undepicted context of his somewhat vengeful forgery.